CW00673110

FALLEN MOON

WOLVES OF THUNDER COVE

CATE CASSIDY

RED SHORE PUBLISHING

Fallen Moon

The Wolves of Thunder Cove

CATE CASSIDY

Fallen Moon © 2021, Cate Cassidy

This story is a work of fiction. All names, characters, locations, brands, incidents, and places are either the product of the author's imagination or are used fictitiously.

CHAPTER ONE

EMBER

The carnival job requirements were simple: turn a blind eye to all sorts of ruthless behavior, always look for ways to hustle, and take as much as you can from each visitor before the day ends.

"Come on, buddy! You can win a unicorn for your girl! Just five bucks for three tries!"

I hated the job, but desperation called for drastic measures, and my rumbling stomach didn't leave me with many options. Neither did the fact that I'd been working these traveling spectacles since I was sixteen.

Sure, I wanted out, but every time I swore it'd be the last time, I'd find myself broke and jobless—having been turned down everywhere else. So, I'd head toward the closest town and take whatever job had yet to be claimed.

Besides, they paid in cash.

"Come on, dude. Break a red balloon, and the large unicorn is yours!"

Of course, it wasn't as easy as it sounded. The gullible folks who handed over their hard-earned cash didn't stand a chance.

The red balloons were practically impenetrable, and the darts? Dull as hell.

"And how much if someone wanted to save themselves the hassle and just bought the unicorn?"

I looked up at the deep voice, and my pulse spiked. To say the man was sexy would have been equivalent to saying the pyramids of Giza were *kinda* cool.

He was gorgeous.

On top of that, he had the bluest eyes I'd ever seen. For a moment, I wondered if he wore fake contacts. But it was the shape of his face that *really* got my attention—masculine planes chiseled to a perfection no man should be allowed to possess, accompanied by a pair of lips slowly turning up into a sexy grin. He reminded me of an Olympic swimmer, all abs and muscle but not the bulky kind.

Stop staring at him, dumbass.

Who cared if he was so...pretty?

Somehow the word didn't seem right considering all that hard flesh; yet at the same time, it suited him perfectly.

But one thing about guys like him was they always knew it, and I hated cocky assholes as much as the next girl.

I shook my head, partially in response to his question but also to shake myself out of my childish stupor.

"Sorry, can't do it. You gotta play if you want any of these stuffies."

His smile turned into a chuckle. "Stuffies, huh? I see. Okay, then." He took a step closer, eying the prizes hanging overhead. "I know she'd love that unicorn."

"Your girlfriend?" The question escaped my lips far too quickly, and any chance of maintaining a shred of dignity vanished instantly. I wanted to slap myself for such thirsty behavior. But instead, I shot him my best phony smile and tried to recover quickly. "If she's here, have her come by and give it a try. I'll even give her an extra shot for free."

I got the sense my reaction to him was something he'd gotten a hundred times before—women gushing over him, abandoning all self-respect just for the chance to bathe in the warmth of his sexy smile.

I was *not* going to be one of them.

At least, from now on.

Yeah, there was no denying that something about this guy turned me on in that first crush in high school kind of way. Gooey, messy, and filled with the promise of regret.

And purely physical, of course. I didn't even know his name.

But I was turning twenty-five in a few months. That was way too old to act like I was still in high school. It was also too old to be working at a carnival, but I tried not to think about that.

He took another step closer so only a couple feet and the waist high, wooden counter separated us. The man was certainly bold. I had to give him that. But even more telling was the look on his face, confidence mixed with something else as though he was enjoying the shit-show—*meaning me*—a little too much.

"I don't have a girlfriend. I was talking about my sister, Trinity." The grin was back, and I couldn't help but wonder if he'd set me up just to see my reaction. "When she was younger, she was obsessed with unicorns. Her room was full of photos, toys..." He smiled, but this time it didn't quite reach his eyes, and I could've sworn he flinched as if he was in pain. "And *stuffies*, as you say."

I narrowed my eyes. *Was he making fun of me?* I couldn't tell.

"So, do you want to play or not? Sorry, I don't have time to stand around talking."

It was a bold-faced lie. I was lucky to get a couple of dozen customers the entire day, despite calling out to everyone who walked by. But that didn't matter. I just needed him to go away so I could quit acting like a fool and get back to work.

3

He nodded, a little too slowly, as though he was studying me and trying to figure me out. Then he took a step back. For a second, I thought I was about to get my wish, and he'd just leave. But then he reached into his back pocket and pulled out his wallet. I caught the flash of washboard abs as the hem of his black t-shirt lifted slightly over his stomach.

Yeah, of course, I noticed.

"Sure, I'll give it a shot." He handed over the money, but I just stared at his hand as though it was a rattler, ready to strike.

"It's only five dollars for three tries. That's a fifty-dollar bill."

He glanced down and then back up at me as though he didn't understand the problem. "Are you able—"

"No, I can't take that, sorry." I knew I was breaking a cardinal rule, but I didn't care. Whenever someone handed me a large bill, I was supposed to take it and then skim on the change. "Do you have something smaller?"

"I don't think so," he replied as he quickly thumbed through his stack of bills. "Oh wait. Here, I've got a twenty."

He blatantly ignored the look of annoyance on my face and held it out to me. "You can just keep the change."

I nodded at the steel contraption sitting off to the side of my booth, securely fastened to the wooden frame. "Just drop it into the box and push down on the handle."

"Got it."

The tray flipped over as he moved the lever, depositing the cash into the hidden compartment below.

"So, here's how it works." I placed the darts on the counter in front of him and tried hard to ignore the intensity of his gaze. "You get three chances. Aim for a red balloon. Those hold the larger prize tickets, which is what you'll need to get the unicorn. Blue ones win you a medium, yellow a small."

"And the other ones?"

I allowed myself to take another good look at him, and when I did, I saw he was wearing a look of amusement on his face.

4

"Nothing. So, red, blue, yellow or—"

"Nothing. Got it." There was that smile again. "Okay, well, wish me luck."

You'll need more than luck, I thought dryly.

I felt a little bad about hustling him. I'd been here all day, and so far, not a single person had managed to break a red.

He lifted the dart from the counter, placed it carefully between his fingers, and moved to the far end of the counter till he stood in front of the giant wall of multicolored balloons.

"Three tries, right?"

I nodded. "That's right."

His eyes glistened in the sun, holding me captive when they seemed to get impossibly brighter. Then, he winked at me, aimed for the wall, and let it go. I couldn't look away from him, despite the dart whizzing through the air.

For a moment, I forgot I was supposed to feign surprise when the tip failed to pierce the balloon.

But when I finally tore my gaze from him, I was stunned to discover he'd managed to land his dart directly in the middle of a now deflated red balloon.

"Try not to look so surprised."

The expression on his face revealed this wasn't the first time he'd made winning a carnival game look like child's play and I was the one who was being hustled, though he'd certainly paid more than enough for the crappy prize.

"Not surprised at all," I replied casually. "So, you want the unicorn then?"

He walked over as I began to climb onto the counter, angling my body so I could reach the stuffed toy.

"Actually," he moved even closer and pointed to a spot in the cluster of prizes right above my head. "I'll take that one."

My eyes flashed to where he pointed. "The gray wolf?"

"Yeah. Is that okay?"

I shrugged and pulled the plush animal from its spot before

climbing down and holding it out to him. "It's your prize. You can have whatever you want."

Instead of accepting it, he stood there as though I had all the time in the world. Then something flickered in his gaze—something I couldn't quite make out, but it certainly made me squirm. And I *wasn't* a squirmer.

"In that case, I'd love to have dinner with you."

Okay, so I wasn't expecting that.

I fidgeted under the heat of his scrutiny, feeling a rush of fire ignite the insides of my thighs. Then his gaze moved lower, like a smooth caress, finally coming slowly back to my face. It was a frank look of admiration, which sent a quiver of heat down my spine.

But there was no way I was having dinner with him. Especially when dinner was probably code for hooking up.

Suddenly, I was way too conscious of how I looked. My t-shirt was just a little on the small side. My jeans—well, my jeans were just as tight, which meant I was probably muffin-topping all over the place. My long, brown hair, somewhat decent when it was combed thoroughly, was likely a ragged mess from working all day. I ran my fingers through it but pulled them back out when I snagged a knot.

No guy had ever looked at me this way before—like he wanted to rip my clothes off and ravage my body. It should've completely freaked me out, but I'd be lying if I said it didn't do something funny to my insides.

Get your shit together. Just say, no thanks.

His expression changed to one of confusion as I stood there staring at him. "Or not?"

"Sorry, I don't eat dinner."

"You don't e—"

"I mean, of course, I eat," I fumbled. "I just usually grab something quick because I'm too tired after work."

I knew I sounded like an idiot, but he'd thrown me a curve-ball I wasn't sure how to swing at.

"Sure, I'd love to have dinner with you sometime."

What. Did. I. Just. Say?

Clearly, my hormones didn't get the memo from my brain that we weren't supposed to be interested.

"Great," he replied, his grin going all dark and sexy around the edges. "I guess I should ask for your name."

"My what?"

"Name?" He regarded me silently for a moment. "I'm Cody."

I forced myself to look away, peering over his shoulder at a group of teenagers who were waiting to board the most nausea-inducing ride of them all, the Spinner.

"Oh, right." I gulped down the ball of nervousness lodged in my throat before making eye contact again. I couldn't believe I'd agreed to have dinner with this guy before we'd even exchanged names. "I'm Ember."

"That's a beautiful name. Nice to meet you, Ember."

I shivered at the way he said my name—growled it more like, my body prickling with goosebumps as if just struck by a gust of chilly air, yet I was the farthest thing from cold.

"And you can keep that." His gaze darted down to the stuffed animal I hadn't realized I was still clutching in my hand. "You know, in both Greek and Norse mythologies, wolves were considered guardians of the gods. Maybe it'll bring you some luck."

"I don't believe in luck," I replied, my voice edged in steel. "And you forgot Fenrir, the ruthless predator who killed Odin. Not to mention Little Red Riding Hood wasn't exactly lucky when she met up with a wolf."

"Touché," he murmured, boldly leaning forward and reaching out to brush a few wayward curls from my face. The ghosting caress of his fingertips left a trail of heat in their wake, stretching from my cheek to my ear.

I stilled at the touch—caught off guard that he was so daring but also at how good it felt.

"Sounds to me like she just met the wrong wolf."

I wrinkled my brow in confusion, but before I could reply, he suddenly turned his attention to something off in the distance. Then his smile disappeared and was replaced by a look of confusion. Finally, his gaze returned to mine.

"I better get going, but I'll be in touch, okay?"

I frowned at his sudden change of heart.

Was he seriously blowing me off after just asking if I'd have dinner with him?

"Don't you want my number?"

Something flickered in his eyes then, but it was gone so fast I wondered if I'd imagined it. "I don't need it." His voice had roughened, deepened. "I know where to find you."

He turned to walk away. But he paused, and I prayed he'd set a date and time, something—*anything*—as a promise, I'd get a chance to lose myself in the depths of his eyes once again. Instead, he murmured something I couldn't quite make out, and then he was gone.

CHAPTER TWO

EMBER

The rest of the day dragged on. I couldn't get Cody off my mind, no matter how hard I tried. Even people-watching wasn't enough to distract me from the memory of his smile. And the couple passionately making out on the Ferris Wheel just a few yards away wasn't making it any easier.

I thought about how long it had been since I'd felt a man's lips pressed against mine. Longer than I cared to count, that was for sure. Let's just say that if we earned points for turning casual dates into ridiculously awkward interactions, I'd hold the top score.

I'd all but given up on love, and that was okay with me. There were other things worth doing in life than falling for some guy.

But if Cody was on a dating app? He would be a definite swipe right.

Still, I didn't like how I'd fumbled over my words and shamelessly flirted with a stranger. Then again, I'd never met someone who'd left me a drooling mess the way he had. A man who was thrilling enough, lovely enough, intriguing enough to make me forget every one of my rules.

And in my world, rules existed for a reason.

But it didn't matter anymore because now he was long gone, and I'd likely never see him again. He hadn't even bothered to take my number.

"Ember?"

I looked up from where I was kneeling, my hands full of the prizes I had to pack up for the night. The carnival was closing soon, so no one was interested in playing games because they were busy trying to get in just one last ride.

"Yeah?"

A tall, white-haired man looked down at me with a scowl as though I was nothing more than a wad of chewed-up gum stuck to the bottom of his shoe. "I'm here to clear you out for the night, girl."

"And who are you?" I stood up, hands on my hips.

A younger man named Gregory had always been the one to collect the cash at the end of the day. I wasn't about to let some stranger snag the little bit of money I'd managed to bring in. I knew better than that.

He held up a key as proof he was meant to be there. "Johnny. I'm Gregory's replacement. He had light fingers if you catch my drift."

"But—"

"I don't have time for this." He moved behind the stand, brushing against me as he walked by, and I scowled.

"Boss said you need to start doing better. If you can't bring in more cash tomorrow, you're done. We're only here for another week before we move on, and at this point, you're just dead weight."

My spine stiffened in annoyance. "There's nothing more I can do. I can't force people to play these games."

"Not my problem. The last guy brought in twice as much. You know how this works."

I watched as he pulled the cash from the box and started to

count it. I knew I didn't bring in as much as I used to, but with diminishing crowds and the fact stuffed animals had lost their appeal ages ago, it wasn't easy to convince people to waste their money on silly games.

I let out a deep sigh. "If that last guy was so good for business, why isn't he here?"

Johnny laughed darkly. I shuddered at the sound, but the words that came out of his mouth turned my stomach.

"He got caught with a minor. Poor guy didn't know she was only sixteen." His eyes darted around, ignoring my glare, and then he found what he was looking for—an elastic band which he wrapped around the thin stack of bills and shoved into his jacket pocket.

"Such a shame. He was one of the best we had. He ran the stands, but he could also repair the equipment when a ride broke down. Unfortunately, the boss had no choice but to let him go."

"He should've been more than fired. He should be in jail," I replied with a sharp edge to my words, my temper flaring. But the truth was, I wasn't surprised. I'd heard countless stories, just like this, and I knew I'd listen to many more.

Johnny cocked an eyebrow and barked out a sinister laugh. "If every guy here got arrested for chasing young tail, we'd be left with... you." He waved his finger at the empty cash box. "And then this would be one hell of a shit show. Do better tomorrow, or you're fired." He threw a few bills on the counter, a day's wage, and without another word, he turned and strode away.

I looked around at the shrinking crowd and sighed. It was likely I wouldn't do any better tomorrow.

I was screwed.

"Don't let him get you down."

I spun around at the sound of the voice and came face to face with a guy who stood at least six-feet tall with a battered, leather pack slung over his shoulder. His dirty blond hair was spiked in all directions, just this side of messy, but in a way that looked as though it was intentional—as if he'd speared his fingers through it.

What was this, bring a hot guy to work day?

It wasn't every day that two handsome strangers dropped by my stand.

"I beg your pardon?"

He nodded in Johnny's direction. "He isn't going to fire anyone."

I blinked. "You know Johnny?"

He shot me a curious look but ignored my question. "I'm sure they know how lucky they are to find anyone willing to work here. It's not exactly a promising career." He chuckled, but his idea of humor was lost on me.

"Obviously not. But it's better than nothing." I replied, slightly insulted by his comment. I didn't need to be reminded of how terrible the job was. "There are worse things I could be doing."

But the truth was, it didn't get much worse than this. I had to deal with the touchy-feely guys who operated the rides, the pickpockets who lurked within the crowds, not to mention my boss, who refused to pay us even minimum wage.

He raised an eyebrow at my sharp response and lifted his hands as a sign he was just teasing. "I didn't mean to piss you off."

I pulled myself up straight, took a deep breath, and started tying up the last few bags of stuffed animals.

"And you're right; there are worse jobs," he replied thoughtfully. "Embalmer, school janitor, not to mention being a proctologist."

What was this guy's deal?

I crossed my arms and quirked my eyebrow. "Is there something I can do for you? If not, I need to finish up here." I made myself busy wiping down the counters, so I didn't have to look at him. I wished he'd just leave, but a few minutes later, he was still there, his eyes sweeping the counter between us and finally settling on mine once again.

"I'm sorry," he replied, offering his hand along with a half-smile that told me he genuinely felt like an ass. "I'm Dawson." When I didn't acknowledge him, he added, "I didn't mean to come across, so, you know, condescending? Rude? Arrogant?"

"All of the above?" I quipped, ignoring his hand as I looked over the stand one last time to make sure I hadn't missed anything. I wanted to get the hell out of here as quickly as possible.

I couldn't help but smirk when he dipped his head to catch my eye.

"Can we have a do-over?"

Fine.

I reached out in response, but I wanted to pull away when my hand touched his. An intense streak—of what I imagined lightning felt like—tore through my body, making me cry out in pain. I fought against the potent current searing through my veins, but I was powerless to it. My head spun as a blur of confusing images raced through my brain.

I tried to pull my hand away again, but Dawson claimed my fingers firmly in a possessive grip. When my eyes met his, I could tell he felt the same strange connection and apparently didn't want to, or just couldn't, let go.

I could barely breathe as the strange flow of energy continued to thunder through every inch of my body. My vision blurred while an invisible force wrapped itself around me.

I tried to focus on his face, but he seemed to vanish, replaced by images of towering trees with pink leaves and silver tree trunks flanking a snow-covered trail that led up to a magnificent castle. Then vibrant bursts of color sailed through my vision—my mind seemingly no longer under my control.

"What just happened?" It felt like an eternity before I could finally regain my composure, but then my bizarre visions sent me reeling backward, everything I'd seen flying by in reverse.

Finally, the pressure in my head ceased, and I yanked my hand from his.

Immediately, I felt better—lighter, as though someone had lifted a weight from my chest, and I could breathe again.

"I... I have to get going," I squeaked, my voice faltering. I peered up at him in confusion, that invisible thread of *I-don't-know-what-the-hell-just-happened* still somehow lingering between us. "I need to get home."

"Wait," he replied, and I couldn't help but notice how his steel-gray eyes lit up. It was as though he'd suddenly uncovered a secret. "Are you okay?"

"I have to go," I replied, ignoring his question and nodding toward the edge of the carnival grounds.

"Hey, hold on. You look like you're ready to pass out. Are you sure you're okay?" he asked for the second time, that knowing expression never leaving his face.

"What?" I tried to remember what he'd just said as I looked around, still in a daze. "Yeah, I'm fine. Thanks."

His look of deep concern told me he wasn't buying it. I probably looked like a raving lunatic to him, but I was still dealing with the remnants of whatever had just happened.

"Why are you here? Where have you been staying?" He must have realized how sketchy he sounded because he quickly growled at himself and took a step back. "I just don't feel right leaving you like this."

I shook my head. "As I said, I'm fine." I opened the side gate and stepped out of my booth, wanting to put some distance between us. "Take care, Dawson."

With a swiftness that startled me, he stepped forward and rested his hands on my shoulders. Thankfully, this time I felt nothing when he touched me. His eyes were steady on mine, but I couldn't quite read anything behind them.

"You really shouldn't be here, Ember. It's not safe."

"I told you, I'm fine." I scowled. "I just need to be left alone."

He raised his hands and took another step back. "Okay, but please be careful."

Unwelcome tears pricked my eyes, and I blinked hard before they could escape as I watched him walk away. I wasn't sure what had just happened, but it had shaken me to the core.

Suddenly, my shitty apartment seemed like a haven, and all I wanted was to be at home, curled up in my bed, where I could surrender myself to the sweet reprieve of slumber.

CHAPTER THREE

DAWSON

I knew she was one of us the moment I felt her hand in mine. The energy that had flowed between us revealed the connection, even though it was one-sided. It was clear she had no idea how to seize control of her real power, which filled me with great sadness and concern.

Her wolf seemed almost...muted.

How was it even possible she'd survived the human world for so long?

Our kind was rarely found outside of our realm, much less in the human world. Not only was it dangerous, but the human world was considered off-limits. There was a long-standing agreement between all shifter clans that we stayed clear of it.

For what reason, I'd probably never know. Legends described the dangers of humans discovering our kind if we roamed freely throughout their world. Some believed the rule existed because of the threat of shifters breeding with humans, thus weakening our race.

Whatever the reason, it wasn't enough to keep me away. I certainly knew of the risks. But there were pieces of our history scattered all over the human world, and I was determined to find every one of them.

Besides, I'd promised my father I'd always take at least three men with me. Just as a precaution.

But why was *she* here?

For a she-wolf, it was nothing short of a death wish.

But how could I explain to her that she didn't belong in this dangerous place and she needed to come home with me where she'd be protected?

My mind raced as I thought about what to do. I couldn't leave without bringing her home with me. I *wouldn't*.

Even if it meant I had to do it against her will. She'd understand later once she realized what she was.

I nodded to the men who'd accompanied me into this world to let them know I was fine but to keep their distance. The last thing I needed was for them to join me and draw attention—nothing like a group of loud shifters to cause a commotion.

Craig, a friend and my future beta who'd watched the entire scene unfold, tipped his head in acknowledgment and then signaled for the others to follow him so they could give me the space I needed while I waited for Ember to finish work.

I weaved through the dwindling crowd, heading to the tent sectioned off for adults, and took a seat on one of the empty stools. It seemed like a good place to lay low—maybe the only place since there were no longer many people on the grounds.

My eyes never left Ember, even when the bartender asked what I wanted to drink.

"Whiskey, please."

I thought about what I should do as he slid the plastic cup across the wooden counter. Maybe a quick shot would help clear my head of the remnants of whatever had happened between us.

I thought long and hard about my options. The portal to my

world was a good half mile away. I had to convince her somehow to head in that direction with me.

But how?

She'd been more than a little spooked by the connection, and if I was honest, so was I. In all my twenty-seven years, I'd never had that happen before.

What did it mean?

I didn't feel she was my mate or anything like that. She was attractive, sure, but I assumed when I finally met *the one*, it would be a very different connection, a link neither of us could ignore.

Or so I hoped.

Not to mention, I hadn't exactly made a good first impression. I'd fumbled for words, asking random questions, as I'd tried to recover from the shock of finding a she-wolf in this place.

"Hey, handsome."

I swiveled to find a buxom blonde with bright red lips sidle up to the bar. She tapped her long, painted nails on the counter as the bartender rushed over to take her order.

"I'll have what he's having."

The bartender nodded and went to work pouring her drink while I ignored the way she leaned toward me, her bare shoulder brushing up against mine.

I wasn't interested. Nothing was going to distract me from keeping an eye on Ember. Besides, the woman wasn't my type.

She took a sip of her drink and let out a whistle. "I must say, I haven't had whiskey in years. Prefer the lighter stuff." She took another swallow and then turned to me.

"What's a sexy fella like you doing sitting here by yourself?"

My body language should've been enough to let her know I wasn't interested in conversation, but she seemed oblivious to that fact. When she brushed against my shoulder again, it was clear she wasn't going anywhere without being acknowledged. I'd just have to make it short and sweet.

"I'm just waiting on a friend." I shot her a tight smile before returning my attention to Ember. Hopefully, that would be enough to shut her down.

It wasn't.

"A girlfriend?" She giggled before ordering another shot. "She's one hell of a lucky girl. You're so hot. I'm sure you hear that all the time."

I said the first thing that came to mind, hoping it would end the conversation, "Trust me. I'm the lucky one. She's one of a kind."

Movement in the distance caught my eye, and I watched as Ember headed toward what I assumed was the main office. She disappeared through the door only to resurface a few minutes later with her backpack.

I turned to the woman as she purred some sexual remark about how what my girlfriend didn't know wouldn't hurt her.

"Hey, I gotta go, but have a great evening."

She scowled as I threw down a bill that would cover her drink and mine, along with a sizable tip. I couldn't lose sight of Ember.

I inched closer, being careful not to be spotted. I expected her to make her way to the main exit, but she turned in the opposite direction and headed for the edge of the forest.

I frowned.

Why would she venture into the darkness of the woods on her own?

I had to be careful. There wasn't a crowd to hide among anymore, and between us was a wide-open space. If she saw me, she'd likely lose her shit. I wouldn't blame her. Seeing a stranger following her home from work would freak anyone out.

I wished I could tap into my magic, but I knew it was too risky.

It was too bad, though. I could be stealthy in my true form. In this form, every step I took felt like a heavy one that threatened to give me away.

I trailed her, keeping a healthy distance between us, yet stayed close enough, so I didn't lose sight of her. I sensed Craig and the others as they started to follow, but I was far enough away not to have to worry about them being able to close the gap quickly.

Suddenly, Ember started jogging. I forged ahead, scowling at the snapping of twigs and the rustle of dry leaves beneath my feet.

"Dawson."

The sound of my name whispered across my skin, and I spun around on my heels, looking for the source, though I knew who was calling out to me. It was the same voice that always beckoned me home after I'd been away for too long.

She didn't care about the dangers of invoking magic from across the realms. She didn't even care that it was magic borrowed from who should've been her sworn enemy. When she wanted me back, she'd risk anything to get her way.

It infuriated me, and I decided I'd finally take care of it once and for all. I didn't need to be summoned by her as though I was still a child under her control.

"Dawson, it's time you returned home. Your father isn't well."

I shook my head as the all-too-familiar shadow closed in. My heart sank at the knowledge my father was ill, but I couldn't leave without Ember.

"Not now. I found someone... one of us. I have to bring her back with me."

I turned back, frantically searching for Ember, but she was no longer in my line of sight. I rushed forward, desperate to find her, but the inky shadows moved along with me, wrapping themselves around my legs and arms, binding me in darkness.

"We need you, my son. Come home."

Panicking, I tried to call out to Ember, but her name was only a strangled cry from lips that were suddenly only half there. My body began to fade, skin turning translucent until I was nothing more than a pale form, a ghostly silhouette that could neither speak nor move.

I closed my eyes, knowing what would come next as my body was transported against my will from the human world back into my own.

Yet somehow, I managed to form the words I hoped would reach her in my final seconds.

Ember.

Ember, you don't belong here. Look for the portal. It'll bring you home.

CHAPTER FOUR

EMBER

My work day was finally over. I pulled my jacket over my head, leaving the hood covering most of my hair, and threw my backpack strap over my shoulder. It was colder than usual, so I hurried along.

My chosen shortcut took me through a forest, but it shaved twenty minutes off the long walk, and as tired as I was from being on my feet all day—and from the strange encounter with Dawson—those extra minutes meant everything.

The sun was dipping below the horizon, so I switched on my flashlight. I might not scare easily, but I certainly wasn't fearless. Every rustle of the tree branches made my heart beat just a little faster.

To distract myself, I thought about Dawson and the strange reaction I had when he'd taken my hand in his. There was no denying that *something* had happened between us.

I wondered if I'd possibly suffered a temporary mental breakdown, and my brain had been unable to process anything. It would certainly explain the weird state I'd been in. Otherwise, I didn't know how to make sense of the overwhelming sensations that had taken over me.

I certainly knew one thing: I *never* wanted to feel that suffocating current of energy—ever again.

Then my mind drifted to Cody as I pumped my legs harder, increasing my speed. He was such a striking man whose bedroom eyes made me weak in the knees. Not to mention, his voice was a gravelly, husky mess that did wicked things to my mind and body. There was no kidding myself; every part of me had been desperately attracted to him.

But somehow, it seemed like more than that, considering I couldn't shake him from my mind ever since.

He'd been charming and warm, but it was as though I'd been looking for someone like him all my life and I just didn't know it.

And the truth was, I didn't.

Love was a foreign word to me, and one that left a somewhat bitter taste in my mouth.

Sure, Cody had left an instant impression on my heart. But so had Dawson, though for all the wrong reasons.

Besides, a heart can only be broken so many times before the scar tissue prevents anything from getting in.

I inhaled deeply, slowing my jog to a brisk walk as my weary body begged for a rest. But, like the sucker for punishment I was, before too long, I was back to thinking about the two of them.

Perhaps I'd fall in love one day and lower my guard for someone. Let someone in.

Maybe—

The chilling realization that someone was behind me made me quicken my pace. My instincts told me not to look back, to just keep running as fast as my legs would carry me.

But it didn't matter how quickly I ran because within seconds, there was a wave of heat at my back just as a sharp pain ripped across my shoulder blade.

A blade.

I screamed as terror set in, and my trembling fingers lost their grip on my flashlight.

I was out here, alone in the dark with a stranger who wanted to hurt me. The warmth of my blood seeped through my sweater, and instantly, fear was replaced by a surge of adrenaline. I tore through the forest, moving from the path to where the brush grew denser.

I needed to find a place to hide.

I pumped my legs as hard as they were willing to go, my hands reaching out to feel my way as I darted under the forest canopy in search of shelter.

With my lungs aching and my body ready to collapse, I lunged behind a massive tree, the cover of its thick, low-hanging branches and giant trunk my only hope of salvation.

Then I waited, shaking while my brain desperately ordered me to quiet my breathing as my heart pounded in my ears.

Silence. Nothing but silence.

Whoever had been right at my heels was gone.

I sucked in a deep breath as the searing pain from my wound came back in full force. I squeezed my shoulder, applying pressure, hoping I could stop the bleeding.

Then I heard it. A soft puffing as if someone was releasing short breaths in quick succession.

Hrmmp...hrmmp...hrmmp.

Whoever it was moved closer, and the gasping intensified. Faster, louder.

Then I realized what the sound was. It wasn't someone breathing; it was someone *sniffing*.

It was trying to pick up my scent.

The scent of my blood.

I muffled a scream and tried hard to focus. I needed to survive, I had to make it out of this forest alive. And above all else, it was imperative that I get myself out of the shadows and into the light. Because light meant people would be nearby, and I wouldn't be out here in the middle of the woods on my own.

The darkness was now my enemy.

I could sense it licking at me, wanting more than a taste, needing to swallow me whole. I felt like I was in the belly of a beast just crouching in the shadows as this sinister force grew around me, thickening with hunger and hate. Then a piercing screech hit my ears as sharp claws suddenly reached out for me.

"No! Leave me alone!"

A searing pain ripped across my throat, and my feet kicked as hard as they could, connecting with a massive, unmovable body. I clamored backward, my hands digging into the ground as I desperately scrambled to my feet and tried to put distance between myself and the massive creature.

Another deafening screech tore through the night, this one louder than before. As my mind frantically struggled to figure a way out of this bizarre situation, I felt the beast move closer.

It came at me again, as if from nowhere, its hulking body towering over me, ready to strike me down. I lifted my hands, trying to protect myself from its assault, but it swung at me, knocking my backpack off and sending me toppling to the ground.

"Help! Please, someone! Help!"

Now was no longer the time to be silent. I screamed as loudly and as long as my lungs would allow, hoping someone–*anyone*–would hear me.

I didn't know whether someone rushing to my aid would even matter though. The beast seemed powerful enough to wipe out an entire town in one fell swoop if it wanted to.

It suddenly dawned on me that it seemed to be taking its sweet time, toying with me, enjoying my torment. There was no denying it could've killed me in a matter of seconds. As tough as I liked to think I was, I was no match for what stood in front of me.

I struggled to get back on my feet. It felt like every inch of my skin was on fire, the wounds burning, though I hoped they were only superficial. That somehow, someway, I could survive this dreadful night.

"What do you want from me?" I shouted at the hideous creature, and for the first time, I got a good look at its face.

Its features were twisted into a menacing scowl, rotting teeth peering out from behind cracking, black lips. And its eyes burned blood red as if all the evil in the world lived inside them.

It didn't speak, didn't acknowledge my cries. It only stared at me with its cruel, curious gaze. It lifted its arm, and I saw the glint of its murderous claws again.

Then, it did the strangest thing. It sniffed the night air. At first, it merely inched closer, its lips curled into a peculiar shape, almost as though it was silently screaming.

My eyes widened when I felt a current of an unexpected gust of wind tugging at my skin and hair. It wasn't strong enough to move me, but as the creature breathed me in, I began to feel lightheaded, almost like I'd faint if I didn't look away.

Somehow I found the energy to make another run for it, desperate to put as much space between us as possible. I was disoriented, not knowing what direction I should be headed for, but I ran for my life.

I wasn't going down without a fight. Especially not by some demonic-looking creature.

I'd come too far to go out like that.

I tried to find the path as I ran blindly through the darkness, my lungs threatening to collapse. I managed to dodge a large tree limb only to fall to the ground as I tripped over a root, my face smashing against something hard. The world seemed to spin, confusing me with sounds and scents, forcing me to scramble to unsteady feet.

Ember.

Someone was calling my name. I wiped the mud and sweat

from my face and leaned against the gnarled tree trunk whose root had caused my fall.

Ember, you don't belong here. Look for the portal. It'll bring you home.

I scrambled across the brush, searching for a rock, anything I could use as a weapon. My head pounded, fear relentlessly scratching at my insides.

A growl, not my own, reached my ears. I blinked back tears, spat out the blood that had filled my mouth, and turned my head at the sound, a whisper of my name once again.

Ember.

It had to be death calling out to me. Whatever came next was headed directly at me. And it was coming fast.

CHAPTER FIVE

GRAYSON

The last thing I wanted to hear about, as we ran to the portal that would lead us to the human world, was Cody prattling on about some girl that he'd met.

Lucky for him, he didn't use the words *fated mate*. He knew I'd kick him in the nuts if he did. We weren't from the generation of shifters who'd been brainwashed by such bullshit. The idea that every shifter was meant to be with just one true mate went against basic biology, for starters.

We were wolves, after all. Fierce creatures designed to explore, to fight, and yes, to fuck. We wanted to find love—of course, we did. Who didn't? But the idea there was only *one* person out there who was meant for us was ludicrous.

Because what if we never found her?

Were we then destined to spend the rest of our lives with battered hearts and broken souls?

No, the promise of every Alpha finding his fated mate was nothing more than a lie told throughout the ages to control leaders, encourage permanence, and pressure pack members to choose a partner merely to strengthen the clan.

And, of course, to keep the lineage going.

Still, fated or not, if an Alpha didn't claim a mate before the end of his first year in power, the pack would question his ability to lead. Most of the elders still believed in true mates and unbreakable bonds. To them, not finding our mates signified weakness, that we were undesirable.

I didn't need a fated mate to help me rule the way the clan was meant to be governed. There were plenty of beautiful women in our territory to keep me occupied.

Still, the faster Alex and I found a woman to rule by our side, the better. It was total nonsense, but it would keep everyone happy.

Cody and I stepped through the portal leading from our realm into the human world, and the bright light washed over our skin, blinding us for a moment before the colors shifted and the ground settled beneath our feet.

"There's just something about her," Cody said as we picked up speed and retraced his steps toward what he said was a carnival of sorts. "I *felt* it. Right away. I felt her wolf, but it was as though—"

"I'm *not* here for a girl," I muttered. "I just want to find out what members of the Silver Creek clan were doing in this world. I don't care about anything else."

"I know," he replied quietly. "And I'm sorry. I know I shouldn't have been there either."

"Yeah, you're right about that," I bit back in frustration. "What the hell were you thinking?"

Cody had been warned too many times about venturing into the human world on his own, and I couldn't let it go this time. Especially now that members of the Silver Creek clan had been spotted in the same area. "That treaty was made for a reason, and we need to abide by it. You're no better than them."

I swallowed a breath of air, making a mental note to start focusing more on cardio and less on weightlifting. I could run for miles without stopping as a wolf, but this broad-shouldered human carcass wasn't nearly as capable.

"It won't happen again, Alpha."

I couldn't help but notice the way his voice cracked when he spoke.

"You know how Trinity is," I replied as we continued moving through the forest. "She always has a nose in one of those adventure books. I'm sure she's just off exploring." I slowed down as the path ahead formed into a T-junction. "Exploring *our* realm, not this place," I added as he stepped forward, indicating which way to go. "She'll come back when she's ready."

In response, he sped up, forcing me to run faster than I wanted to. I was about to yell at him to slow down, but he suddenly came to an abrupt halt, causing me to nearly crash into him.

"What the fuck, Cody?"

But one look at him, and I saw that something had caught his attention. There was a dark glint in his eyes as he scanned the growing darkness of the forest. I'd seen that expression before, and it always meant trouble was on the horizon.

"Did you hear that?"

I listened intently to our surroundings, but the sound of an owl off in the distance was the only thing I heard. Then again, I knew my senses weren't quite as sharp as his were. He had a keen knack for detecting things beyond even the most skilled shifter's ability.

"No, I didn't hear anything," I replied, squaring my shoulders and turning my senses outward. I was about to tell him that we needed to keep moving when I finally caught a hint of what he'd detected, and we both answered my question at the same time.

"Dark magic."

Cody stepped forward, ready to go to battle against whatever was lurking in the shadows, but I reached out and gripped his shoulder.

"Wait." When he shot me a questioning look, I knew what he was thinking.

How could he not rush into battle to destroy an enemy and protect his Alpha?

After all, that was what he was trained to do. Protect his Alpha at all cost. His fierce loyalty was just one of the many reasons we'd made him our beta when Alex and I had taken our rightful places as Alphas.

As the scent of dark magic grew stronger, even I had to fight the urge to shift and chase the shadows until I had its throat between my teeth.

But we knew one thing, and it held us back from shifting. Dark magic didn't just show up in the human world without cause. The evil skulking in the shadows was here with a purpose. Someone had called on the darkness to do their bidding.

"We should head back."

"But what if this thing follows us, Grayson?" Cody asked, suddenly dropping all formalities.

As one of my closest friends, I preferred to keep things as they always were—just two old comrades, equals—but the reality was, it was no longer the case. I was an Alpha, and Cody was my beta. And in turn, we were both painfully aware the clan expected him to always address me as such.

"We need to get out of here. We'll send word to Silver Creek that we want to meet with them on our territory and find out what they're up to. This isn't a coincidence. One of them must have caused some trouble and summoned this creature from hell." I cocked my head to the side, suddenly wondering if I was blaming the wrong person. "Unless you did something—"

"No, of course not. I was just here looking for my sister. As soon as I spotted Silver Creek, I took off before they could see me. I came right back to our realm to let you know."

"Good. Let's go."

Cody nodded in agreement. Despite wanting to charge into the shadows, it was clear what I'd said made sense. We couldn't be sure what we'd be up against. It was just too dangerous, even for us.

"I wish we could just fucking shift. I feel so damn weak like this."

I puffed out a breath in frustration. "Even if we could, two of us against whatever hell just unleashed isn't a chance I'm willing to take."

"Make that three of us."

I turned at the sound of a familiar voice as Alex appeared behind us, deep lines of worry creasing his brow. "You shouldn't have left without letting me know. If Rylen hadn't seen you two headed for the human portal, I would've never been able to find you. You know the rules. We can't be here."

I frowned. I wasn't surprised to discover my fellow Alpha had followed us, but I wasn't thrilled with his decision to leave our clan. It was an agreement we'd made months ago—one of us would always stay behind so as to never leave the pack unprotected. Apparently, he thought he'd be more useful with Cody and me than back in our territory, but I wasn't sure.

"What is that?" Before Cody or I could respond, Alex cocked his head to the side, and it was clear he sensed what had stopped us in our tracks. "What the fuck?" He gazed at me sideways through his tumble of black hair, eyes filled with accusation, but I shook my head in annoyance.

"Wasn't us," I replied. "Silver Creek probably stirred up trouble. This is why none of us should be here. You never know what'll happen in this shitty world."

The forest rumbled with another sound, but this time it wasn't from some wicked beast lurking in the shadows. It was the cry of a woman, and by the sound of it, she was pleading for her life.

This time, Cody didn't wait for a command from his Alphas. He took off running in the direction of the sound, and we knew we had no choice but to follow. We picked up speed, matching his stride, Alex just a beat ahead of me.

"We can't just rush in", I tried to tell them. "What if it's a fucking trap?"

They were both ignoring me, their determined gazes locked on the path ahead, but I wouldn't let up. They were acting reckless, and while I expected it from Cody, I certainly didn't think Alex would forget the clan depended on us to lead so he had no business chasing after some unknown creature.

Or a woman.

No matter how much she needed our help.

"This isn't our responsibility, Alex. Our job is to lead our clan, not save the human world from whatever the hell is out there."

"A woman is in danger," he replied. "You, of all people, know this is the right thing to do. We can't just leave her to die." He turned to look at me briefly, but he seemed to know better than to say what I knew he was thinking. "I couldn't live with this on my conscience."

I hadn't lost my so-called humanity, as Alex liked to say when we were in the middle of an argument. What I *had* lost was the freedom to take chances and to think only of myself.

Becoming Alpha meant I was to always put my clan above all else. They were all that mattered, and I'd do everything in my power to lead them as well as my father had.

And that *didn't* include chasing down some monster to save a damsel in distress.

Besides, the human world had nearly cost me everything many years ago. If it hadn't been for Cody spotting members of Silver Creek, I would've never entered through the portal again.

We heard screaming once again, but to my surprise, Alex and Cody slowed their paces. I hoped they'd come to their senses, knowing it was best we returned home to our pack. But to my dismay, Cody yanked off his t-shirt. It hit the ground as the animal inside him began to surface.

"No! Cody!"

But it was too late. I turned to see Alex was following suit, not even remotely concerned I wasn't happy about it.

I watched in annoyance as their bodies twisted and contorted, muscles stretching as bones grew and thickened. Fangs and claws replaced teeth and nails, feet and hands grew thick gray pads. And last, always last, was the tail.

Of course, I knew we were much stronger in our true forms, but tapping into our magic in this world could make things a lot worse, especially if a human spotted us. They tended to shoot first, ask questions later.

Still, they'd left me no choice.

I quickly undressed, kicking off my jeans, and gave my wolf what he wanted most, permission to be free. The sensation of him rushing forward and taking control was always my favorite part.

Second only to being with a woman, nothing felt better than the surge of adrenaline mixed with the sheer power of my beast. It never got old.

But at that moment, I didn't have time to enjoy it as dark thoughts rattled through my brain. With only three of us ready to face some unknown creature, I couldn't help but wonder if I'd be alive tomorrow to feel the shift again.

I only hoped this woman was worth saving.

CHAPTER SIX

EMBER

Death was but a few feet away.
Every movement, regardless of how small, sent a surge of horrifying pain through my limbs, but I knew I couldn't give up. I couldn't surrender to whatever darkness lived in this forest. I had to keep fighting.

But I didn't have the strength to run anymore. My body betrayed me as it refused to lift from the ground, and I knew I was losing too much blood to hang on much longer.

Then it happened.

Three streaks of fur flew past me into the dense brush, chasing after the creature who'd attacked me.

I was still breathless and weak from fighting its razor-sharp claws, but I managed to pull back a shred of my hoodie to examine the deep gashes that wound down my shoulder and arm.

My stomach lurched at the sight, but I had to stop the flow.

"Let me help."

I scrambled backward, catching my tattered clothes on a branch and crying out at the pain tearing through my body.

A God of a man—naked, muscled, and squatting offered me

a look at the goods, *and damn were they impressive*—smiled at me like all was perfectly normal here, nothing to see. But obviously, there was.

None of this made any sense. I wanted to scream for help once again, but I knew no one would hear my cries. Fear and panic took over, making me forget all about the pain.

The stranger reached out to me, and I shrieked, swatting at him. He was tall, and his chest and arms were covered in tattoos. With his broad shoulders and high cheekbones, he reminded me of a Viking warrior.

"Don't touch me!"

"I won't if you don't want me to, but we can help." He tilted his head as another equally tall and naked man appeared from the edge of the woods.

"Please, let us take care of you."

I was speechless and paralyzed. The leaner one was telling me he wanted to help, but he was *naked*, in the middle of the forest... in the dark... with another man. My mind raced in fear, my breathing frantic and my body a tangle of nerves. But I had no choice but to listen to what they had to say, if only long enough to find a way out of this.

And if they did want to help me, maybe they had a phone to call an ambulance. But if so, Lord help me if I could guess where they put it.

"Let us help or bleed to death—the choice is yours." The tattooed man's expression was all matter of fact, though he worried his bottom lip. "Yeah, we're naked, but there's no time to explain right now." He reached out slowly. "Is it okay now? To touch you."

His amber eyes were kind despite his intimidating stature and were outlined by short, dark lashes. Wordlessly, I nodded and let him touch my arm where the most damage was.

"Did you see—" I paused. *What did I even say?* They'd think *I* was the crazy one, and they were naked in a forest, so that was saying something. "Did you see... anything in the woods?"

"Just try and calm down. Focus on your breathing," the other man replied. His hair, black as midnight, framed his handsome face, and when his gaze met mine, I could see warmth behind his green eyes that glinted in the moonlight.

He knelt beside me and helped me sit back up as he held my arm steady.

And blatantly ignored my question.

Behind me, another spoke. "Oh, thank God, you're okay."

I located the source of that deep, resonant voice—somehow familiar, and when it finally came into view, I gasped. "Cody?"

He'd been in jeans and a t-shirt earlier. Not naked and disconcerting.

"Hey, Ember," he replied. "Please, try to stay calm. As Grayson said, we can help. You have to trust us. I know I don't exactly look like one right now, but I'm a doctor." He glanced at the two men and then back at me. "And yeah, we saw it."

Their grand plan involved bringing me somewhere with them so they could help me recover. None of it made any sense, so I wasn't going to go willingly. I needed to get away from these men who, for whatever reason, were out in the forest at night nude.

Besides, I'd watched my fair share of horror flicks, and this seemed like the perfect start to a dark and twisted tale where I was the stupid girl who did everything possible to get herself killed.

I'd already messed up by wandering into the forest alone. I wasn't about to make another mistake.

"I'm not going anywhere with you." I struggled to get to my feet, but the sharp pain blazing across my body was too much to bear, and I crumbled under the agony.

Cody was by my side in a second. He wrapped his hand around the worst of my wounds, applying pressure as the guy with the shaggy, dark hair ripped a strip off my shirt to use as a tourniquet.

"Alex, place that just a bit higher," Cody instructed him. "A couple of inches from the edge of the wound. Closer to the heart."

I cried out when Alex squeezed the band around my arm so that Cody could use a stick to twist it tighter.

"I'm sorry. I know it hurts." Cody's expression was filled with empathy. "Take a deep breath."

The third guy, the largest of the three, peered down at us as though he had no idea what to do. So far, other than asking if he could touch me, it seemed he was content to stand around with his perfectly chiseled body until someone tasked him with a job.

"Grayson, go find our clothes," Alex said after he and Cody finished using a windlass to increase the pressure.

There it was, his task at hand. He nodded in response, but the shadow that crossed his face told me he wasn't used to taking orders. Still, he took off running, disappearing into the shadows.

Cody returned his attention to me. Just as before, despite the pain rattling through my body, I was mesmerized by the bright flecks in his eyes.

For a moment, the ache faded, and I was reminded of childhood summers at one of the many foster homes, where there was no better way to pass the time than lying on the grass, staring up at a cloudless sky.

"Ember, you have to come with us."

"I don't have to do *anything*," I bit back, though my tone held no power. "I just need...to get home. Then...I'll be fine."

I knew how outrageous I sounded. But despite the agony of what I was sure were broken bones and the deep wounds that wouldn't stop bleeding, I wasn't about to trust three strangers.

Alex sighed, and his shoulders rose and fell before he replied, "You know that's not true. You won't be fine. Not if we leave you like this. "

"He's right," Cody added. "And no one will be able to help you but us."

"And why is that? Because of that creature?" I tried to focus on staying calm and not lashing out at these men who could easily take me against my will, but my temper got the best of me. "Or...because of the wolves?"

Instead of answering, they shot one another an unreadable look, and I got the feeling when they did speak, they would choose their words very carefully.

"You never have to be afraid of wolves." It was Alex who spoke first as he gave me a strained smile, showing off his perfect teeth. "They would *never* hurt you."

I took a deep breath, trying to find my voice, but it was fading fast. "And that other thing? The creature?"

Cody bit his lip, tension tightening the corners of his eyes. "We took care of it."

I felt drained of all remaining energy, barely able to muster the strength to speak, my words nothing more than a whisper, "You... you killed it?"

Before I could ask them another of the many questions racing through my mind, Grayson reappeared, this time fully dressed in a black t-shirt that strained against his large frame and low-slung jeans that clung to his muscular thighs.

"We should get out of here," he said as he handed a shirt and pair of jeans to Alex, then tossed a bundle of clothing over to Cody, who nodded in agreement before he peered back at me, his expression bleak.

"Ember, we have to go. If we..."

His lips kept moving, but I could barely hear the words as darkness closed in around the edges of my vision. Yet even in my weakened state, I somehow managed to stay coherent long enough to allow his voice to reach me one last time.

"Stay with us! Come on, Ember, open your eyes. Your wolf is stronger than this."

CHAPTER SEVEN

DAWSON

"What do you think you're doing?" I couldn't stop my feet from pacing the full length of the large foyer, rage burning through every inch of my body. "You have *no* right to force me back here whenever you feel like it."

"I understand you're angry," my mother replied. She took a tentative step forward but hesitated. She knew better than to try to embrace me when I was this furious. "But you know how important you are to the future of this clan. Leaving on yet another adventure to a place you have no business going is *not* how a future Alpha behaves."

"You used magic to bring me back," I growled. "You know how dangerous it is to use magic there. You could've killed someone. And my men! They're still in that place."

The look on her face told me she wasn't concerned with the aftermath of invoking magic in the human world—or that my men had been left behind.

It took everything I had in me to hold back from unleashing the flurry of low-blow comments begging to escape my lips as I continued pacing. In response, she let out a sigh of deep frustration before continuing to criticize me, but her words were drowned out by my sea of thoughts.

I needed to get to Ember. I refused to let one of our own wander around the human world for one more day without knowing the danger she was in. Humans, for the most part, weren't aware of our existence. They'd been told throughout the ages that our kind was nothing more than a myth, a ghost story shared to keep children in line.

But it wasn't humans I was worried about. Even if they did discover our existence, there would be very little they could do to us. They were the weaker species, lower on the food chain than they could ever imagine.

And it was a good thing because one thing I knew about humans from my time in their world was that their egos were bigger than those of the Fae.

And *that* was saying a lot.

No, it was something far more powerful and deadly which caused me to worry my bottom lip as I wore out the floorboards.

"I met someone… a woman," I grumbled, mainly to myself. "She belongs here where she'll be safe. She's one of us, but I don't think she knows it. I got the feeling she hasn't shifted yet."

I stopped pacing long enough to let one of Mom's many housekeepers scurry across the room, disappearing into the hallway toward the kitchen. "She can't be left there on her own. Eventually, her wolf is going to surface, and she won't know what to do."

This time I let my mother's voice reach me, but not because I particularly cared about her opinion. I loved her, but she'd gone too far this time. Being overprotective is something most mothers couldn't control. I understood that, but she couldn't have it both ways. She liked to remind me of my future place as Alpha of the Silver Creek clan, yet she treated me like a child whenever it suited her.

I'd had enough.

"Dawson, just because she's a shifter doesn't mean she belongs to this clan. There are many others. Like the Thunder Cove clan, for example. And who knows how many exist in other worlds we haven't yet explored? She could belong to any number of those."

As always, she smoothed her hair and straightened her posture when she was losing her patience. My mother's role as the Alpha's mate was one she took quite seriously—something the clan respected—but why that meant always looking like she'd stepped out of a fashion magazine was beyond me.

Describing my mother as posh would be the understatement of the year.

I wished, just for once, she'd drop the charade and be herself. A woman who didn't place a value on others purely based on their lineage. Someone who felt deep concern for a young shifter wandering around a treacherous world, unaware of the dangers surrounding her.

At least, I wanted to think my mother was capable of feeling emotion outside of worrying about her reputation. Still, perhaps this was it— the *real* Mrs. Alastair—as shallow as a pixie's wishing pond.

"Why does that matter? Even if she doesn't belong to our clan, she's a shifter. She certainly doesn't belong in the human world. Surely father will agree."

Mentioning my father was my go-to defense whenever disagreeing with my mother about practically anything regarding clan business and, in many cases, personal business. I was grateful he was always willing to listen to my concerns, and he rarely refused my requests. In fact, the only time he'd fiercely opposed me was when he'd learned I wanted to explore the human world.

But after I'd shown him Grandpa's private journal that was left to me, he eventually changed his mind.

Of course, my mother didn't know about his change of heart, nor would she. My father made it clear it was to be kept between the two of us for reasons I didn't know, nor had I questioned.

I couldn't blame him for initially being opposed to my explorations, just as I understood why my mother would go so far as to seek the services of a witch to keep tabs on me.

Yet I couldn't seem to stay away. I was born to explore, to quench my thirst for adventure. I blamed it on inheriting my grandfather's restless spirit and the countless stories he'd shared with me about his travels long before he was forced into a role he never wanted.

A role I also didn't want to inherit but knew was inevitable.

Added to that, his entries describing hidden relics and buried artifacts that once belonged to my family, and it was all I thought about. Every time I found a hidden treasure, it filled me with such pride to know *I* had reclaimed a piece of our history.

But the treasure I wanted to find more than any other was still lost to me, buried somewhere in the human world. One of the last clues was a faded entry that revealed it would be the most powerful asset our clan would ever recover, hidden away in an eastern town in the human world.

And that was what had led me to the carnival grounds.

"Your father won't be pleased you've been away so long, especially when he's so ill." Her expression darkened as she stared me down. "You should be ashamed of yourself."

That was the gut-punch she'd been saving for just the right moment. When I didn't respond, she mistook my silence as my surrender before switching to her other favorite game, playing with my love life.

"Isabella came by while you were away. She was hoping to spend some time with you." My mother raked her perfectly polished fingernails through her long, red hair as she peeked at me for any sign I'd changed my mind about the woman.

I hadn't.

Isabella was a beautiful shifter and someone I'd grown up with, but she wasn't meant to be my mate. I knew it as sure as I knew my own name. My heart didn't beat for her in that way.

"Stop trying to play matchmaker," I growled. "You're terrible at it. Isabella and I are just friends, and that's all we'll ever be."

My mother nearly rolled her eyes in annoyance. "That's because you haven't given her a chance. I don't understand what you're waiting for. She's a perfectly suitable mate, and her family comes from a long line of powerful warriors. Not to mention, they own quite a bit of territory that would prove useful."

Perfectly suitable.

That wasn't how anyone should describe the person they were supposed to love until their last breath. Yet as far as my mother was concerned, the sooner I chose a mate, the better. I knew she was worried my father would pass on before I'd found my fated mate, but if she'd resorted to encouraging my child-hood friend, she was getting desperate.

Poor Isabella, I thought. She was likely under a lot of pressure to put herself in my line of sight, especially with a family like hers who craved power more than anything else.

I left the room and headed to my father's chambers, leaving my mother behind to pout. I needed to see how he was doing. I prayed he would recover just as he always had. He was the greatest leader our clan had ever known and one of the strongest warriors in our history.

Surely he could survive another bout of whatever this was.

But as I opened the door and stepped inside his room, my heart broke into a thousand pieces. He looked like nothing more than a shadow of his former self. A ghost of a man, faded and withering in a bed that seemed too large in contrast to his crumbling frame.

My father had been known for his brute strength and intimidating stature, but the man lying just a few feet away wouldn't scare off a fly.

Suddenly, I was filled with remorse for being away so long. It was clear he was fading fast, and I'd squandered so much of the precious little time I had left with him.

Perhaps my mother was right. I was selfish and irresponsible for leaving. I should've been here, by his side, doing all I could for him.

"Father, I'm home." My voice came out raspy, my throat tight as I swallowed down the pain of seeing him this way. "I'm sorry I've been gone so long."

I reached out, taking his hand in mine. It was cool to the touch, and for a second, I thought I was too late. That he was already gone. Then he squeezed my fingers, so gently for such a giant of a man I had to blink back tears. His breath was weak, but his lids fluttered open, and I was greeted with the dark gray eyes of a king. Eyes much like my own.

"Dawson," he replied, his voice barely above a whisper. "Back from another adventure. Did you bring back more of our history?"

I frowned. I'd been gone so long only to come back empty-handed, which made me feel even worse. I didn't even have a story to share with him. He always seemed to enjoy hearing about my travels.

"Not this time, father." I sat down next to him, his gaze never leaving mine. "But I think my attention should be here, with *you*. With our clan. I'm not going to leave again. History isn't as important as the present."

My father sputtered out a breath but then seemed to pull energy from out of thin air as he shook his head and squeezed my hand even tighter.

"Quite the contrary," he replied. "By learning about our past, we can lead our clan to a better future. And you're going to be a great leader."

Even in his weak condition, I was sure he sensed how unhappy I was at the thought of becoming Alpha. I didn't want that life. But he also knew I'd never turn my back on my duty to lead.

"I'm glad you have faith in me. I'm not always sure I have what it takes. I have some rather big shoes to fill."

That brought a smile to his lips, but his eyes lost some of their sparkle. It was as though their color was fading with every passing minute.

"Some of us follow in the footsteps of our fathers out of duty, others out of pride. You..." He chuckled softly, and the sound was music to my ears. "You follow the beat of your own drum. Don't ever stop. Not for me, not for your mother...not for anything. It's what will make you a great leader."

He choked out a breath and then sputtered out a string of words so faint I could barely make them out at first, but as I drew closer, I caught enough to understand.

In his final moments, he wanted me to know all his secrets—all the things an Alpha could never share with another in his lifetime, but who needed to clear his conscience before he left this realm for the heavenly one.

I listened silently to his confessions, and in those final moments, as he looked at me not as my Alpha but as my father, I knew this was the end of his long and faithful reign.

He would be gone sooner than either of us was ready for.

He knew it, and as I watched him struggle for another breath, I could no longer deny what I knew to be true.

"I love you, Father. I only hope I can be half the leader you are."

It wasn't easy to sit there and watch my father in his final moments. The little boy in me—the one who grew up thinking my father was invincible, the hero in all my childhood stories—wanted to run out of the room and shield my heart from the painful image before me.

But I wasn't that little boy anymore. I was a man who needed to be strong. To be selfless. To carry the clan's good name as my father had.

To honor his memory.

As the energy in the room shifted like the changing winds at sea, and I watched the air slowly leech out of my father's sail, I held onto him while he took his final breath.

Then I allowed that little boy to surface just one more time as I was swept away in a sea of sorrow, tears falling down my cheeks, my vision becoming blurry. I stayed there for a time, adrift in my heartache and memories, my hand refusing to let go of his.

I wasn't ready. I needed him just a little longer.

But when my tears had finally dried, I gave his hand a final squeeze and let go.

My adventurous spirit would have to die with my father. There were far more important things to contend with now.

I'd walked into the room as a man with an unquenchable thirst for exploration, but I would leave the room a very different person.

I would leave as an Alpha.

CHAPTER EIGHT

EMBER

*M*y blood soaked into the forest floor, dripping off the root that *had broken my fall.*

The voices around me meant nothing, but their faces did. One face closed in, his lips parting, ready to share our first kiss.

I woke to dark curtains letting in only a weak beam of moonlight. My heart suddenly galloped in fear, and I touched my cheek, my shoulder, the arm I knew had been pierced and bleeding. Nothing. I couldn't even feel a scar.

Had it all been a dream?

No.

I threw back heavy blankets, climbed down from the bed, and knocked something over in my race to the windows. But when I pulled back the curtains, the only thing I saw bathed in the moonlight was an unfamiliar rose garden and a fountain glinting with its swift water coursing over what looked like the copper patina of some ancient wolf statue.

This was no place I knew.

"How are you feeling?"

I spun around at the sound of a voice I instantly recognized and glared at Cody, who stood in the doorway looking way too casual for my liking. I'd nearly died at the hands of some creature and then woke up in a strange place. I needed answers, not the sexy smile he shot my way as he stepped into the room.

"How do you *think* I feel?" My tone was unmistakably biting as I spit the words at him, and I felt a twinge of guilt when I saw him flinch.

"I know you've been through a lot, and it's going to take some time to—"

"To *what?* Come to terms with the fact there are monsters? *Real* ones? Or come to terms with the fact you guys just happened to be in the area when it attacked me? What should I start coming to terms with first?" I shook my head in frustration. "None of this makes any sense. And I'm fully healed! Like, how is that even possible?"

His gaze lowered to my arm, and his lips curved into a smile that lit up his face. "I'm happy to see you've fully healed. I made an ointment for you, and it seems to have done the trick."

"Where am I? I don't understand what's going on."

He stepped forward, closing the distance between us, and I felt the weight of his hand on my shoulder just as I had before. I wanted to stay angry. I did—though I didn't exactly know why I was so upset at him— yet his touch was somehow comforting.

"You've been here for a few days, Ember. It took some time to heal."

I gaped in complete disbelief.

Had I really been in this bed for days?

"I know it's confusing, but it'll all make sense soon. One way or another, we'll figure out what happened."

His face revealed he wasn't so sure what he was saying was entirely true. He shrugged at my questioning expression.

"Or maybe it won't make sense." He exhaled deeply as if he suddenly realized no matter what he said to me, I'd never understand. Then he took a step back, retreating, though he kept his hand on my shoulder. "Maybe you'll think we're just crazy, and there'll be no changing your mind."

"Quite likely," I replied and watched his expression grow somber. "But I still want to know."

"We don't have all the answers…not yet. But we'll never lie to you." He paused and waited until I was looking at him. "I'll tell you everything I know. And as unbelievable as it may sound, Ember, it's real. All of it. So please, at least be… open-minded."

I took a step back. Suddenly, I needed space, as though being merely touched by him had turned my mind to mush, leaving my scattered thoughts to float through my brain aimlessly.

I also needed answers and a clear head. Not to be transfixed like a pathetic girl with a silly crush on a boy. A guy I didn't even know. But the burning intensity in Cody's eyes was hard to ignore—almost impossible—even if I was in an unfamiliar place with a stranger and should be focused on getting the hell out of there.

Yet, somehow, he didn't feel like a stranger at all.

"So when do I get some answers then?"

Cody ran his fingers over the stubble on his chin, but before he could respond, the other two men from the night of my attack sauntered into the room. Alex looked troubled, but Grayson stood back against the wall, seeming as though he could care less about any of this.

"Did you…"

Cody shook his head. "No, not yet. I was waiting for you."

From his corner, Grayson surveyed me as though I was nothing more than an intruder in their home. "What do you want to know?"

Where did I begin?

I tried hard not to rapid-fire my questions, choosing instead to start with exactly what went down before I was brought here.

"What happened in that forest? And why am I here?"

And the one question I didn't dare ask.

Who are you guys, and what do you want with me?

Grayson sighed as if my questions were nothing but gibberish. "Why don't you clean yourself up, then meet us downstairs? There's a lot to go over. And we have questions for *you* as well." He nodded toward the large closet which ran the full width of the back wall. "Cody bought you some clothes. You'll find everything you need in there."

"Wait," I tried to sound braver than I felt and braced myself for whatever they were about to throw at me. After fighting off the creature in the darkness, nothing should scare me. Yet, I felt my chest tighten with anxiety at whatever truth they were about to reveal. "Please. Just tell me everything."

I didn't miss the way Grayson shot Cody an *I-told-you-so* look, but all I cared about was that he'd do as promised and give me the information I so desperately needed.

Alex stepped forward, this time taking my hands into his and gently pulling me over to the bed. "You may want to sit for this."

I didn't fight him on it. I sank down, and he took the space next to me. "So, the creature who attacked you that night," he began, and I could tell he was trying to soften his voice. "We don't know why it was there or why it attacked you. It isn't from the human world. Cody and I have done some research, and we believe it's from the realm of shadows."

I shuddered at the thought of the strange beast, and I grimaced. "Realm of shadows?"

"Yeah, a world of dark magic."

My stomach twisted. Now I knew these men were bullshitting me.

"You're out of your mind," I replied. My gaze shifted from Alex to Grayson and then settled on Cody, who'd barely said a word since the others showed up. "All of you. You're crazy."

He stepped forward hesitantly, and for the first time, I realized just how tall he was compared to the others. "Alphas, if I may." He waited for them to nod their approval. "Ember, it's true. I know it's a lot to take in, but there's more to the world than what you've known. There are two worlds, yours, a world of humans…and ours, a world of magic. And that creature, let's just say it came from somewhere in between."

Grayson smirked when I didn't respond. It was apparent he was annoyed by my reluctance to believe what they were saying. There was no denying a monster had tried to kill me, but a world of magic?

"Yeah, I wouldn't believe it either," he grumbled, gritting out the words. "But you either believe us, or you'll likely be dead when you return to your world. It's up to you."

Alex shot a fiery glance his way before sitting next to me, his expression somber.

"Ember, I know it's a lot to take in, and we're not making things easier to understand, but we're trying." He glanced around the room briefly before his eyes met mine again, and for a moment, I felt how tortured he was. "Like Cody said, the world we live in… it isn't the world you know. This place…" He lifted his hands up. "Is a shifter realm. Our town is called Thunder Cove, and it's one of many in this world. It's where magic lives."

This time, I couldn't help but laugh. I didn't mean to, but the words coming out of his mouth sounded more than outrageous. They sounded like the murmurings of a madman.

"Where magic lives? As in witches and warlocks and sorcery? Ooh, and goblins?" I knew my tone was a mix of disbelief and sarcasm, but they couldn't possibly expect me to believe what they were saying.

Alex lowered his eyes, and it was clear he had a lot more to say. I braced myself.

"Yes, witches and warlocks and sorcery. As well as Fae and—"

"Shapeshifters." Grayson crossed his arms over his chest. "Like bears, dragons, and wolves, just to name a few. The wolves you saw the night you were attacked, for example, they were shifters."

"Shifters." I caught all their gazes in turn before continuing, "The wolves who chased the monster away... were shapeshifters?"

Grayson snorted. "She's finally getting it."

Alex shot him a dark look, but it didn't seem to faze him. "Yeah, they were shifters."

"And that thing? That creature? What was that? A shapeshifter as well?"

"No, it was definitely not a shifter," Cody replied. "*That* was dark magic, and as we said, it was summoned by someone or something. I know it sounds hard to believe, but it's true."

"In other words, *you* did something to piss someone off, and they sent that thing to kill you," Grayson grumbled. He slid his hands into the front pockets of his jeans and shrugged, drawing attention to his broad shoulders. "I have my ideas about how that, but this guy—" He tilted his head toward Alex. "—doesn't seem to want to listen."

"Not now," Alex bit back. "We'll talk about that later."

"No." I shook my head in frustration. I needed to know everything. Not bits and pieces, but every single detail. "You say that monster was there to kill me because someone summoned it." The silence stretched a few seconds. Frustrated, I stood up and faced them. "You're saying you think someone wants me dead?"

Alex eyed me carefully. "Yes, that's exactly what we're saying."

I swallowed hard. "But I keep to myself. I don't have enemies."

Grayson shrugged. "Clearly you do."

My mind raced, and a wave of nausea hit me like a ton of

bricks. "Maybe you're wrong, and that creature was just there, in the forest, waiting for the first person who ran by."

"No," Alex sighed, and I could see he was struggling to find the words—to help me understand. "Like I said, Cody and I found references to that kind of creature in the archives. Those things only appear when a magic-user summons it to do their bidding...to destroy an enemy."

"I just don't understand why anyone would want to kill me." None of this made sense to me. I was a nobody. I'd been on my own for years, minding my own business, living my life completely alone, staying off anyone's radar. I certainly wasn't special. And I didn't have enemies. "Tell me what I need to know."

I peered around the room, trying to make eye contact with them, but no one seemed to want to acknowledge my request, much less look me in the face.

Finally, Cody turned to me, and our eyes locked, his bright and burning with an emotion I couldn't quite read. "From what we've read, depending on the target, a different creature is said to appear. One designed to destroy a specific kind of magic." He shrugged. "Again, this is only what we've been able to uncover so far. There isn't a lot of information about this."

"The kind of creature who attacked you is called lupus interfectorem," Alex added. "It's one of the more powerful shadow creatures."

My brain drowned out the rest of what he was saying as I tried to wrangle it around the words he'd used. The language sounded familiar, but I couldn't place it. I tried to repeat the phrase, sounding them out. "*Lupus interfect—*"

"It's from the old language," Grayson cut me off.

His tone made the little hairs on the back of my neck stand up.

"It means wolf slayer."

CHAPTER NINE

GRAYSON

There was no fucking way she was meant to be in this realm.

Yeah, she was beautiful with the curves of a Goddess, but who cared? It wasn't enough for me.

It was clear her wolf lay dormant, having never felt the wind on her back. There was no denying shifter blood ran through her veins. But if her wolf had never awakened, what use would she be to us?

She was a halfling, of all things. She just had to be. If she was a full-blood, she couldn't have denied her wolf for so long. It made her beyond weak. Certainly not someone we should've risked our lives to save.

I knew from the look on Cody's face he disagreed, but he knew better than to argue with me.

One thing was clear, he wanted her to stay—the way his body stiffened around her as if it took every ounce of strength not to reach out and comfort her said as much. But if she was just a halfling, he'd never be able to claim her as his mate. Still, the way his eyes roved over her body told me if given a chance, he'd sweep her off her feet, take her home with him, and make love to her for hours.

Or maybe more my style—fuck her hard against the wall, on the floor, and in the shower.

That I could get on board with if she was a full-blood. It had been quite some time since I'd felt a woman beneath me, and it was long overdue. But a *halfling?*

Not a chance in hell.

Not to mention, she'd be seen by our clan as nothing more than an abomination if they found out that she hadn't shifted yet. I wouldn't allow my beta to destroy his family name just for a piece of ass.

Even one as deliciously curvy as hers was.

I glared at Alex, hoping my fellow Alpha would at least acknowledge that this woman we'd risked our lives for was nothing more than a problem we now had to get rid of. Then he could help me talk Cody into bringing her back to her own world.

Why would the universe, fate, the shifter gods, whoever the hell was responsible for our hearts connecting with another, ever lead Cody to her?

What did he ever do in his life to deserve that?

Not to mention, she was impossible. Despite how she tried to keep her shoulders square as though she could handle anything we told her, it was clear she was overwhelmed.

Cody deserved a strong partner. Every shifter did. Someone who could stand by our side and take on the world with us. Not some weakling who looked like she might pass out from stress at any minute.

I scratched my head in frustration. We'd already told her what we knew about the creature who attacked her, but we hadn't told her *why* Cody was gawking at her like he'd never seen a female before.

When I looked his way, ready to just lay it all out there and tell him there was no chance Alex and I would allow her to stay, I could tell from his expression he wouldn't take it well. Of course, he'd know there'd be no sense in arguing, but nothing could create a rift between friends like a woman could.

I didn't understand why he'd even want her when there were so many beautiful she-wolves who'd die for a chance to be his mate. After all, Cody's looks made women want to drop their panties and rub up against him like naughty kittens, begging him to make them purr.

I was disappointed. I wanted so much more in a mate, and so should he. A woman who'd become a part of me, the missing puzzle piece, my twin flame.

And she was certainly *not* that.

"But obviously, I'm not a wolf." Her voice had suddenly grown quiet, barely above a whisper, and I could tell she was trying to make sense of why a creature known for killing wolves had been after her. "If I was, how could I not have felt *something* over the years?"

The truth was none of us knew the answer to her question. It was clear we all felt the stirrings of her wolf, but it was nothing more than a faint pulse of what should've been a skilled and powerful creature. Ember had to be in her twenties. If she hadn't shifted by now, chances were she never would.

"You'd think so," I replied. "But maybe being in the human world just fucked all that up. No wolf could survive there."

I moved closer to where she was sitting, wanting her to listen carefully.

"Ember, there really *are* two worlds," I began, trying to keep my voice as steady as possible even though I just wanted to roar in frustration when she cocked an eyebrow at me as if to say she thought I was nothing more than a rambling lunatic. "Yours and ours. Right now—" I waved my hands around the room to emphasize what I meant. "—you're here, in *our* world. A realm of shifters that's hidden from humans. Follow me?"

Cody crossed his arms over his chest, and I got the sense he wasn't happy with the way I was talking to Ember. But I was more than a little discouraged by how complicated this had gotten. Like a mass of crossed wires we had to untangle carefully for fear of setting off an explosion.

We'd known about how the world worked since we were born. We were taught about the many realms and the magical creatures who existed in each one.

But Ember? Up until now, she'd never even imagined such things, much less had so much happen to her in such a short time.

"I know what you're trying to say," she replied, crossing her arms. "It just all sounds so unbelievable."

"I know." Alex nodded. "It's a lot."

"Especially when you've never even fathomed any of this before," Cody added defensively. "Humans have no clue there's an even bigger world of magic with potentially hundreds of realms and portals."

"Portals," Ember said the word as though she was testing it on her tongue. "I heard one of you mention that the night I was attacked. You told me to look for one. That I didn't belong or something. I guess it makes sense if you think I'm a wolf."

Alex shot us a look which said whichever one of us had said that shouldn't have. But when I cast a glance at Cody, he shook his head.

"Someone told you to look for a portal?"

She wrinkled her brow in confusion as she tried to unravel all her tangled thoughts. "Yeah, I heard a voice telling me to look for the portal. Wasn't it one of you guys?"

I shook my head. "No, it wasn't us."

"Magic exists," she continued, ignoring my response. She spoke slowly as if processing everything she'd been told one measure at a time. "And you brought me here through a portal."

Cody reached out and squeezed her arm affectionately. "Yes, that's right."

She worried her lip as she turned to me. "And you think I'm somehow magical. Like a shifter because of the kind of creature who attacked me."

I shrugged. "Appears that way."

"We have some business to take care of." Alex abruptly stood and strode to the door as if he was afraid asking her anything about her wolf would send her over the edge. "When you're done showering, come downstairs, and we'll have dinner. You must be starving."

Ember frowned. It was clear she still had so many unanswered questions, but apparently, Alex thought we'd done enough talking for the time being.

I disagreed. *Why drag this on?* We ought to tell her what she needed to know and then let her have a meltdown so she could go back to her world. We had more important things to do—like leading our clan, forging agreements with other packs, expanding our territory.

Things far more beneficial to our pack than lusting after some *mostly* human woman.

Cody mumbled something about how he'd see her later. Then he and Alex disappeared through the door, leaving me alone with Ember.

"Hey." I kept my voice low, steady. "I know it's a lot to wrap your head around. They just don't want to overwhelm you."

"They," she repeated. "But you... you'll tell me everything."

It wasn't a question.

I shrugged. I had nothing to lose. As far as I was concerned, the sooner Ember returned to the human world so we could get on with our lives, the better.

Then maybe we could start focusing on finding our real mates.

"Then tell me." She narrowed her eyes. "Tell me everything

you know. Like why you guys were in the forest that night. And why you brought me here."

A creature had tried to kill her days ago, and now she was in a strange place, learning magic existed and she had a wolf living inside of her who hadn't awakened. I had to give it to her—it was a surprise she could even form a coherent sentence at this point.

She got to her feet and moved to the window, where she slowly parted the curtains. My heart galloped in my chest at the idea she might see Alex and Cody roaming freely in their true forms, needing to relieve some of their tension. But before I could shield them from her vision, she sucked in a breath, and I knew she'd spotted them.

"Wolves." It was a breathless statement, as the pieces of the puzzle finally began to take shape in her mind. "There are wolves out there. Two of them."

She spun on her heels, her eyes filled with accusation. "And *you*. The wolves...the three wolves who attacked the creature. Who saved me. They were—"

"Yes," I replied, holding her gaze.

Her face darkened.

"That was us."

I expected her to scream, to bolt for the door and try to put as much distance between us as possible, but she remained rooted in place. The expression on her face was unreadable, but I didn't miss the way she bit her bottom lip.

"Have you always been a shifter?"

Her question caught me off guard. She wasn't screaming for help or attempting to make a run for it.

"Yeah, of course." I nodded my head toward the window. "You don't get turned into one. It doesn't work that way. Everyone in this realm is a shifter."

Her lips curved into a hint of a smile. "Well, not *everyone*. At least, I've never felt any sort of magic."

"Right, well, like I said, I have some ideas about that."

"And what are those ideas?"

"*We* can all feel your wolf... but barely. I think the human world subdued her somehow, especially if you've been there all your life." I paused as the scent of her wolf suddenly grew stronger. "Besides, if you weren't a wolf, you wouldn't have been attacked by that creature, and you also wouldn't have been able to go through the portal with us."

"I see," she replied, her gaze never leaving mine. "It's shocking, that's all. The fact that all of this is real... *Magic*... I mean, who would've thought?"

"Did you honestly think your world was the only one in existence?" I asked, trying to lighten the mood. "From what I've read, humans are always looking up at space, trying to find signs of other life, imagining other creatures are out there. They don't realize we're right next door."

She cocked an eyebrow. "But even if humans did believe, they wouldn't be able to pass through a portal into this world, right?"

"True," I replied, stepping back and leaning against the wall. "Yet you're here, and I don't think you're a full-blood, so who knows?"

"So, you think I'm some half-wolf. Like, a mutation?"

I cleared my throat. Suddenly having to explain that, yes, we believed she was some sort of half-breed, not a full-blood, felt more than a little awkward. Like I was about to tell her she was a disgrace to our kind—a living, breathing scandal.

Because the truth was, that was exactly what a halfling was. And there was no way our clan would ever accept her. She had to go.

"Mutant, no, but you're definitely not one of us. If you've never felt the pull to this realm and you've haven't shifted by now, you can't be a full-blood. You're a mix of wolf and human or something."

There, I'd said it. I just hoped Cody would face the reality she wasn't meant to be here so she could go back where she belonged. Besides, there was nothing we could do for her. She'd managed to survive for her entire life in the human world, so she'd be just fine. Sure, she'd somehow pissed off a supernatural who'd summoned darkness to destroy her, but it wasn't our problem. She'd have to figure it out for herself. We did more than enough by saving her life. Not to mention bringing her here and nursing her back to health.

At least that was the partially formed game plan struggling to emerge from a storm of wicked thoughts.

Thoughts I shouldn't have had as I surveyed the smooth curve of her shoulders which led up to a dainty neck. My gaze tracked to a pair of plump, pink lips I wanted to feel wrapped around my—

I chastised myself for letting my mind wander to places it had no business going while she regarded me silently for a moment before she pivoted from me, staring back out the window.

"It's honestly kind of exciting," she replied. "I've read my share of paranormal books, but never in my wildest dreams would I have ever imagined any of it could be true."

"Paranormal books?" The idea she was equating us to outrageous horror stories of haunted houses and moaning ghosts more than pissed me off.

"Paranormal romance, mainly." She smiled shyly over her shoulder, and it made my pulse spike. She seemed so sweet and innocent in that moment, yet something underneath told me she'd seen her share of dark days.

"A lot of people read them." The words were rushed as if she felt the need to validate herself. "You guys said your world is full of different types of supernaturals like witches, warlocks, and of course, shifters..." This time, she turned fully around to face me, and the look of excitement on her face made me smile, despite myself.

"Yeah?"

She paused briefly, obviously contemplating whether to ask me the question or not.

"Just ask me, already."

Her gaze clicked around the room before settling on me. "Are vampires real?"

I didn't know what I expected her to ask me, but it certainly wasn't *that*.

"Yeah, they're real." Before she could say another word, I rolled my eyes. "Whatever you've read in those romance novels, believe me, they're nothing like that. They're ruthless killers. We steer clear of their realms."

"Realms? So, they have more than one?"

"Unfortunately, yeah. They're always at war with someone, usually one of the Northern covens, and when they conquer, they take over the realm."

"And who are *your* enemies?"

"We try to stick to ourselves, but we've seen our share of battles. Not all clans are satisfied with their territories, and they want more. Most often, we're our own worst enemies." I let out a whisper of a sigh at the memory of those we'd lost over the years.

Brothers, cousins, close friends—all lost in a vicious battle against greed and dominance.

But it was losing our fathers that hurt the most.

"Some of the greatest leaders we've ever known were taken from us by clans who desired power over anything else. My father was one of them." I took a deep breath. "Alex's as well. They were true warriors who would've done anything to honor their pack, including putting their lives on the line. I won't let our clan ever forget them."

I didn't know why I told her all that, but once the words were out, I couldn't take them back.

Suddenly, it felt as if the air had been sucked from the room as I watched her face light up with a sense of understanding.

"I'm sorry, Grayson." Her gaze was steadfast in its intensity and compassion.

I struggled to draw a breath as I took her in, my confession hanging between us. Desire and longing suddenly filled my body again, and it took everything to fight off the need to wrap my arms around her. In that instance of weakness, my attempt at not wanting to acknowledge she was different from anyone else we'd ever met came crashing down.

It shouldn't matter if she was a human, a shifter, or possibly something in between. She needed our help. There was no way she'd survive another year if we sent her back to the human world. Not before her wolf had awoken.

Her cheeks turned pink, and she dropped her eyes. I could barely contain myself—my muscles taut, my heart pounding, my cock hardening. I wanted to do much more than console her and tell her everything would be okay, assure her she was safe here. I wanted to rip our clothes off and feel her skin against mine. My wolf nearly howled at the thought of wrapping my arms around her waist, setting her on my lap, and burying myself inside of her.

Fuck it.

There was another beat of silence, and then I stepped forward, closing the distance. I reached down, brushing my knuckles over her cheek. I was ready to kiss her, to feel my tongue inside her mouth and her curves in my hands.

But somehow, I managed to control the desire threatening to take me to a place of no return.

"Get cleaned up and then come down and eat," I murmured as I felt the heat of her body so close to mine, beckoning me.

No matter what I wanted, she wasn't mine to claim.

She bit her bottom lip and lifted her eyes to mine, and it was clear she felt it too. Before I could say or do something I'd regret, I spun and strode away, leaving her alone with her thoughts.

I suddenly understood why Cody had been treading so carefully. Maybe he was right. Maybe we didn't need to rush into things. She'd already been through enough for one day.

Besides, she wasn't going anywhere anytime soon.

Ever, if Cody had anything to say about it.

CHAPTER TEN

EMBER

R *un!* The word on repeat was all that had been in my mind since Grayson shut the door behind him.

It had taken everything in me to hide the swell of panic that coursed through my veins when they'd tried to explain all the craziness they'd concocted.

Magic, shapeshifters, wolf slayer.

They were insane. There was no other explanation, but the only thing I knew was I wasn't about to stick around and find out just how much worse it could get.

What was their plan for me? To keep me captive? To use me as some sort of sex slave?

A million thoughts raced through my frantic mind until finally, their words had become nothing but a tangle of murmurs as I contemplated my escape. Thoughts of leaving inevitably led to thoughts of the three men who'd rescued me. Especially the surly one.

Grayson. Something had changed in his demeanor. He'd momentarily let his guard down when he'd talked about his father, a stark contrast to the aggressive, moody side he seemed to be more comfortable with. When he'd touched my cheek so gently, I'd felt how vulnerable he could be, and it did something to my insides. But he was also intense—so many confusing and complicated layers.

But none of it mattered because these guys took the definition of unstable to a whole other level.

I'd been scouting for a way to get out of this strange place from the second Cody and Alex had excused themselves. When I'd moved to the window initially, I'd figured my only escape route was through it, but when I saw the wolves roaming free a story below me, I second-guessed my chances of making it out of there alive. They looked fierce and wild.

Think, bitch!

I took a deep breath. Something tugged at my memory like a word stuck on the tip of my tongue, refusing to surface.

I'd gotten myself out of some dangerous situations before, but *this* situation was a lot more complicated. To start with I didn't even know where I was, and from the look of things through the window, the grounds were massive, meaning I'd either get lost or end up a wolf's dinner.

One thing at a time. Get out, then find your way back home.

Unfortunately, after searching the connecting rooms and only finding a massive walk-in closet and a beautifully decorated bathroom—both of which had no exit—it was clear my only option was through the bedroom door. Once out in the hallway, I'd look for a way out, try to stay away from wherever they might be, and get outside. From there, I'd run as fast as my legs could carry me, avoiding the wolves, and make my way back into town.

And from there, well, I wasn't sure, but I'd worry about that later.

Plan made, I crept up to the door, pressing my ear against the dark wood. I couldn't hear any of them, not even a distant murmur. Opening it slowly, I prayed it wouldn't creak, and to my relief, it didn't. I took a step out into a long hallway, the glossy marble floor leading out on both sides of where I stood. I spotted a rather grand staircase to the right, trimmed in gold ornate and what looked like black, iron spirals.

I headed toward it, willing my steps to be as light and quiet as possible. My gaze clicked around. I could either go down the winding staircase and take my chances they wouldn't be downstairs, or I could go through a large set of double doors at the end of the hall, just a few feet away.

The sudden sound of heavy footsteps was unmistakable. Someone was coming my way.

So, I hurried through the door, closing it softly behind me and sidestepping along the wall. The room was filled with several large easels. Dozens of paintings and half-finished canvases were scattered all over the place, as though whoever had created the art was more than a little irritated the pieces hadn't turned out the way they'd envisioned.

I quickly made my way to the other side of the space, spotting yet another door. My heart pounded so hard in my chest I thought I'd faint, but as I turned the handle and saw it led outside, the breath I was holding in burst free.

I swung the door wide open, and then raced down the stairs to the ground below. I was outside. Now all I needed to do was figure out which way to run so I could put as much distance between myself and this house as possible.

Cautiously, I slid against the brick wall until I got to the very end, then peered around the corner. To my dismay, the bright sun overhead was suddenly swallowed by dark clouds. Off in the distance, I heard the deep rumbling of thunder, a sharp contrast to the piercing screech of the creature who'd tried to kill me a few days ago.

I bristled with fear at the memory. I'd been sure I was about to die. Then the wolves had appeared. The men who brought me here claimed those wolves were shapeshifters. And that *they* were those wolves.

I steadied myself, drawing in another deep breath as I tried to collect my scattered thoughts. I had to get out of this alive.

There were three of them, wolves roaming free, and only one of me. I didn't like the odds.

A howl sounded as I took a tentative step forward, and that was when I saw it.

A wolf.

I'd never seen one up close before, so I never knew just how large they were. Looking at them from above was one thing, but having one just a few feet away from me was more than a little terrifying. Its coat was a dark gray, and it was silvery-white on its underbelly and hind legs.

My mind recalled my neighbor's Golden Retriever, but I quickly pushed the thought away.

This creature was *not* at all the size of a Golden Retriever, which was how I'd imagined wolves until now, like fiercer versions of man's best friend.

But this wolf probably had no friends at all, and if he did, man certainly wasn't one of them.

I slowly retreated, heading back toward the stairs. Maybe I could get back to my room before any of the men came looking for me, and then I'd have time to strategize and figure out a better way to escape. He snarled, so I tried to talk to him in soothing tones, saying the first thing that came to mind.

"My, how big your teeth are. Hope not the better to eat me with."

I didn't know what I expected to happen after saying something so foolish, but the wolf moving into a flattened position and whining wasn't it.

It watched me ease away slowly, creeping up the stairs. It only perked its ears when I tried the handle on the door to the room I'd been all too happy to escape through moments before he showed up.

I tugged on it with all my might, willing it to open. The sound of footsteps behind me made me jump.

A naked man appeared, all hard muscle and swagger. When my eyes met his, my heart raced up into my throat.

Cody.

"If you're looking for Grandma's house, you went way off course." A smile tugged at his lips. He clutched a scrap of fabric in his fist.

"Please, Cody. I need to get home." My brain tried to make sense of what had just happened, but it quickly gave up. "I don't belong here."

"Ember, relax. You're safe here. I promise."

Why had my world turned upside down suddenly?

Then again, it wasn't as if it had ever been smooth sailing. I guess I shouldn't have been surprised my luck would lead me into some elaborate prank with a trio of maniacs.

"I understand how confusing this all is," he continued. "I can't imagine being in your shoes. I wish we could make it easier for you."

"But you could," I shot out angrily, my mouth dry. "Just let me go home."

"If only it were that simple." There was a pause, and then he peered around as though he was searching for someone to help him explain. When he realized it was just the two of us, he straightened his shoulders. "Listen, if we let you leave, you'll be in danger. We don't want that." He strode forward, staring down at me without touching me. "And I'm sure you don't either. We can protect you here."

"I'll be fine."

He couldn't possibly expect me to trust three strangers who'd been talking in riddles since I woke up in this peculiar place.

"I'll go to the police. And I'll tell them about the attack. They'll send a unit out to search the forest, and they'll find whatever it was."

Cody's gaze clouded over into a grim expression. He slipped on a pair of shorts that did little to conceal him. "The police won't be able to help. They wouldn't believe you, and you know it. Even if they did, humans wouldn't even be able to see the creature when it came after you again."

"But *I* saw it," I replied through gritted teeth. "And despite what you say, I'm *not* magical... I'm certainly not a wolf."

Cody didn't move, but I got the feeling he wanted to touch me. Perhaps shake me into understanding his warnings—knock some sense into me. But it would take more than that to convince me any of this was real.

That thing had hurt me, yes, and it had felt very real in the moment. But the logical part of my brain still struggled to come up with an explanation. Perhaps, it was a man in a mask or costume—a crazed serial killer on the loose.

Anything else made sense.

Anything else, except that the creature was somehow super-natural.

Anything other than the idea *I* was supernatural.

I believed in many outrageous things, but magic and monsters were too far of a stretch, even for me.

"You're not entirely human, Ember. If you were, that thing wouldn't have attacked you. And you wouldn't have been able to go through the portal with us."

His words hit me like a freight train, pummeling my chest so hard I couldn't breathe. *Yet why did I react that way?* Grayson had already said the same thing to me a few minutes ago.

It wasn't like I suddenly believed them.

Or did I?

The fact only a few minutes ago, there was a wolf where

Cody now stood didn't escape me. Still, it wasn't like I'd *seen* him shift.

I sucked in a breath. "I'm obviously *not* a wolf." I lifted my arms to emphasize I was made of normal human skin, not fur and fangs. "So, what am I? A witch? A goblin, perhaps?"

He smiled at me again. It was somehow a relief to see the corners of his mouth lift. Somehow his smile told me he'd help me figure it all out.

"First, you're way too cute to be a witch or a goblin." He eased forward. "And second, you really shouldn't run from me."

"Should and will." My words felt thick and slow, with no more power behind them than those shadows of tree limbs flailing on the wall beside him.

"Will you, Ember? Will you run?"

His gaze held me there with my back against the door, his expression telling me things that heated my face, things that tingled along my hungry skin and pooled at my core. He took another step forward, closing the distance.

I was no longer sure I had the energy to run, but I knew I most definitely should.

He ran a hand along my collarbone, and I practically lost the ability to stand.

"I don't want you to leave, Ember. Stay with us. At least until we figure things out."

I shrugged. "I'll just wait until I get another chance to make a run for it."

"Can't let you do that." He put a hand on either side of me, planted firmly against the brick wall. "We want to help you."

"Let me go, please." I planted a palm against his bare chest and trailed it lower, unable to resist. "I just want—"

"I know what you want." He dipped his head and brushed his lips against my neck. "But I need you safe... with me. Please stay."

My cheek brushed against the stubble on his face, a counterpoint of prickly sharpness, contrasting with all the smooth,

73

sensual heat surrounding us. Right then, only the warmth of his body existed. His mouth opened slightly, and despite myself, mine responded immediately. My lips parted, allowing his tongue to meet mine. The urgency of his kiss, the longing... I felt it, loud and clear, right down to my toes as the strength of his body pressed against me.

Then the sky split with a light so bright I saw it behind my closed lids. The crack of thunder followed a second later, and the heavens opened, pouring rain on us. He didn't let it affect what he was doing, clinging to my body with his strong hands and finishing what he'd started.

"Come back inside." His voice, deep and low, was stern. If I hadn't been standing so close to him, I wouldn't have heard him at all.

"No, no...I need to go home, Cody. I can take care of myself." My voice caught, emotion overwhelming me.

"Ember." My name was barely a whisper on his lips, but it shot straight through to my core, igniting a fire I didn't want to put out.

A smoldering sexuality radiated from this man—a sexuality he took no effort to hide—and I was drawn to him like a moth to the brightest flame.

"I care about you, and I'm not willing to let you put your life in danger." He moved a step closer, pinning me under his gaze. Then he leaned forward as he brushed his lips against my neck. "Quit being so damn stubborn."

I opened my mouth to protest, to ask him how he could care for me when we barely knew each other, but his lips found mine again, silencing my words. Then I felt his smile against my mouth before he lifted his head and peered down at me. In the gathering darkness of the storm, his face was cast in shadow, but I could feel a change in his body, his arousal intensifying, matching the rising tide in mine.

"Come with me," he whispered into my hair as his fingers raked the waves at the nape of my neck.

I nodded, reluctantly stepping back. He'd tied my stomach up in knots and set my heart beating like a caged bird who was finally set free.

It was yet another reason to run and never look back.

So then, why didn't I?

CHAPTER ELEVEN

EMBER

My attempt at escaping had ended with me in Cody's arms, his lips claiming mine in a way that left me wanting more. When he'd finally released me, he'd asked me to come back inside. Despite myself, I let him take my hand and lead me into a large sitting room where the others soon joined us.

"Ember, we don't want to hold you against your will—" Cody started.

"Yet you are."

"Please, listen." He crossed the room and sat down next to me.

I couldn't help but notice the way my body responded to him. My shoulders relaxed, and I got the sense if I wasn't careful, I'd allow myself to snuggle into him. The memory of his lips on mine made my body burn with desire.

"Cody, I *am* listening."

"You can leave if you want to."

When I raised an eyebrow as if to challenge him, he shrugged. "Really, you can go. But you should at least learn how to connect with your wolf first."

"And control her," Grayson added.

I lifted a hand. "Don't you think if she's never surfaced before, chances are, she never will?"

Grayson side-eyed me as he shuffled closer, taking up space on the sofa across from me. It was clear he was thinking the same thing. I was almost twenty-five years old. Surely if I had a wolf living inside of me, she would've shown her face by now.

"How old were you guys when you first shifted?" I asked.

"Usually, the first shift happens around ten or eleven," Cody replied. "Though it can take years to learn how to control it, especially during different phases of the moon." His gaze shifted to Grayson briefly, his expression one of sadness, but it was gone before I could blink, replaced by the same intensity as earlier. "And you're right. If you've never felt your wolf before, maybe you never will. But *we* can feel her. That energy... that power. It's right there, under the surface. Have you never really felt it?"

My instinct was to say no, but something gave me pause. All my life, I'd felt different, but not in the way I imagined having a powerful wolf living inside of me would feel like.

If it was true, she was just as fucked up as my human side because I certainly could've used her help throughout my life.

I thought about the years spent in foster homes where I was jostled around from family to family because they thought I was nothing more than a weird kid, and no one wanted to deal with that. I was a loner, anti-social, and always angry, but it came with the territory. I was a walking, talking stereotype, and I knew it.

But how did the saying go?

What doesn't kill you makes you stronger?

"I've never felt it," was my simple reply. "Not once."

"Bullshit," Grayson replied. "You've felt her, and you know it. But you either ignored her or being in the human world damaged her somehow. I know you had to have felt her throughout your life."

This time I had a much stronger reaction. "You don't know *anything* about me. If I had felt her, I'd say so. And all this..." I stumbled over my words, trying not to say the ones that popped into my head, such as stupidity, insanity, and craziness. I didn't want to insult them because it was clear they believed what they were saying. But telling me I was lying about not feeling some *animal* living inside of me was just... "stuff." I took a deep breath. "All this stuff about me being half a wolf and half-human just doesn't make sense to me."

"If you say so."

My skin grew hot. There was no stopping the train of anger that had left the station. "Grayson, if I had *any* idea, I'd have done everything possible to reach her. She could've solved quite a few problems for me."

His eyes darkened a little, but he didn't look away. "I'm sorry to hear that."

I shook my head. "Don't be. Just tell me everything I should know, and I'll deal with it."

"Well, the Fallen Moon is in a few days," Alex said. "There's no better time for your wolf to introduce herself."

My brow furrowed as I tried to figure out what that meant. Many of the paranormal romance books I'd read referenced the moon and its impact on shifters, but I didn't recall reading anything about a Fallen Moon.

"It only happens once every decade or so," Cody explained. "It's when the moon is at its closest point to Earth, so shifters are at our strongest then. Our elders believe it's a moon sent to us from our ancestors to remind us of who we are." He looked over at Alex, a thoughtful expression on his face. "You're right. Her wolf won't be able to deny its pull."

I fidgeted under the scrutiny of their gazes, contemplating what they'd just said. At this point, they could've told me that unicorns were flying across rainbows outside the window, and it wouldn't sound far-fetched.

I made a mental note to ask them later if such wondrous creatures existed.

I cleared my throat, breaking the uncomfortable silence. "Does it hurt? The shift? Seems like it would. All those bones stretching and changing shape and all that."

Before they could respond, there was a knock on the door, and a few seconds later, a giant of a man with a long shock of golden-colored hair walked into the room, carrying a folder in his hand. He surveyed us as if he was trying to assess the mood before speaking.

"Everything okay?"

"Yeah, we're good," Alex replied. "Ember, this is Rylen, one of our betas. Rylen, meet Ember. She was asking whether it hurt to shift."

My gaze flickered to the stranger, who smirked. "It doesn't hurt at all. Quite the opposite."

I let out a breath as my body relaxed. Then another question popped into my head. "Beta? So, a clan has an Alpha and betas?" I side-eyed Rylen and found him staring straight ahead. It was clear he was deliberately avoiding my gaze.

"Some clans have just one Alpha, but we have two. And yes, we have several betas who help us manage the clan. Cody is our first in command, and Rylen is our second," Grayson replied. "That means Cody would take over with leading the clan if something happened to Alex and me."

"And they're also two of our closest friends," Alex added, shooting Grayson a look that made it clear the men were far more than subordinates.

Rylen cleared this throat. "It's an honor to serve you both and to be a member of this clan." He cast a glance my way, and when he spoke, his voice seemed to lower an octave, "And it'll be my pleasure to serve you, if one of my Alphas chooses you as their mate. You would be of great importance to the clan's future."

I couldn't help but notice the way Grayson's body tensed. "Cody is the one who was drawn to her. Not Alex and—"

"*Mate?* Importance to the clan's future?" A laugh rose to my lips, but the look on Grayson's face cut it off.

His gaze was locked on me and was filled with a fierceness that took my breath away.

"No way," I managed to murmur. "Fated mates… that's a real thing?"

Cody shrugged, an elegantly simple gesture for such an important question. "Shifters often choose a mate based on who'll strengthen the pack. Sometimes it's political. Other times… well, there are lots of reasons. Not every member of the clan believes they'll find their one true mate."

"Do *you* believe in fated mates?" I asked, not letting him off the hook.

He took his time responding as though he was second-guessing his response. If we were texting, I would've been staring at the chat bubble forever.

"Everyone wants to believe there's someone out there who's meant for them. Humans like to believe in soul mates. Well, some shifters like to believe in fated mates. It's pretty well the same thing."

I nodded but said nothing. I didn't want to miss a word.

"So yes, I have faith I'll find mine." He leaned closer to me. "I have a feeling she isn't far away." His breath tickled the hair along my hairline before his lips brushed my ear.

Then he stared at me, and I saw he had questions of his own, maybe more than I did. Questions that might lead down a very different path.

I reluctantly slid away from the heat of his body, wanting to clear my mind. He had a way of jumbling my thoughts, and right now, I needed to focus.

"So, how is a mate so important to the clan's future? It sounds like a lot of pressure."

"An Alpha's *true* mate could handle it," Grayson replied. "And before you ask, no, I don't think there's only one person in the entire realm who's meant for me. If fated mates are a real thing, then they're as rare as a red diamond." He paused and peeked at Alex out of the corner of his eye. "Alex and I don't have the time to wait around for that. The clan expects us to choose mates soon."

"And we will," Alex replied quietly. "Relax."

For some reason, the idea of either feeling forced into choosing a mate just because the clan expected it saddened me.

I redirected my attention to Rylen, who seemed like he wanted to bolt from the room rather than talk to me. With his stiff words and equally tense posture, he clearly didn't like the fact I was in his realm, much less my line of questioning.

"And what do you think, Rylen?"

The expression on his face confirmed my suspicions. If annoyance and disapproval had a baby, that's what it would look like.

"I'll be happy for my Alphas, no matter what mate they choose. It will only strengthen the clan."

And the lie detector has determined that was a lie.

"Okay, so what now? I wait around for this Fallen Moon and then see if my wolf makes an appearance? And after that, when I want to head back home, you'll help me get there?"

"If you still want to go, then, yes. As I said, we would never keep you here against your will," Cody replied.

Grayson cleared his throat, drawing my attention to his curious expression. "Are you close to your family? Because if you go back, you know you can't tell them about any of this."

I frowned. Not because I wouldn't be able to tell anyone, but because I had no one to tell. I'd been a one-woman show for as long as I could remember.

But did I want to tell these men no one would be looking for me?

My mind raced. Perhaps this was the perfect opportunity to make them think people would be searching once they found I'd disappeared.

I opened my mouth, ready to tell them my lie, but something made me hesitate. I didn't know if it was the flicker of desire that crossed Cody's face or the way Grayson stared at me like he was struggling between not wanting to give a damn about what I decided and something else—something deeper.

Or, maybe it was because I felt like there was more to me than just broken bits and pieces for the first time in my life.

These men believed I had some hidden power, and they wanted to help me connect with it.

Whether it was true or not, I couldn't be sure, but what harm would it do to stick around for a bit?

If nothing else, it sure as hell beat working at the carnival. I could use a break from ordinary life. And when I ignored the crazy talk that came out of their mouths, I had to admit, the way they looked at me didn't make me feel like they were threatening or deranged. Something about them made me feel at ease, like I'd known them for years.

"No, I don't have any family, and don't worry, I wouldn't tell anyone about any of this."

Alex opened his mouth to say something, but Rylen stepped forward, scrubbing his face with the palm of his hand as if he had bad news to deliver. "I brought a copy of the agreement, as you requested." A black inked tattoo showed on his left wrist when he held a folder out for Grayson to accept. "Is there anything else I should do before the meeting on—"

Grayson lifted a hand. "As a matter of fact, yes. There are a few things we need to talk about before those pricks step foot onto our territory. Alex, Cody, we should head over to the meeting hall and hash this out."

Rylen's gaze clicked over to Alex, silently asking him

whether Grayson was about to lose his cool. Alex tilted his head in a way that seemed to give Rylen the answer he was looking for.

"Do we really need to do this tonight?"

Grayson glared at Alex as though his question was ludicrous. "Members of the Silver Creek clan will be here a few days after the Fallen Moon to discuss the agreement, and apparently, their new Alpha wants to discuss changing it. Don't you think it's something we should fucking discuss before…" He took a deep breath before he continued, and when he did, his voice was far gentler, "It won't take us long."

"Of course, Alpha," Rylen nodded, heading toward the door. "Should I call the others?"

"No," Grayson replied. "Just us four for now. I want to keep this under wraps. Those bastards have a lot of explaining to do, but so do we." He looked at Cody, his eyes burning with accusation.

I wondered what they were talking about, but it was clear they didn't want to discuss it in front of me, and I wasn't about to ask questions.

"It'll be fine," Alex added, wanting to diffuse the situation. "We'll figure it out."

Cody reached out and squeezed my hand before standing up. "We won't be long. Why don't you take a shower, and then we'll cook dinner as soon as we get back? You must be starving."

"Sure. Sounds great," I replied.

They made their way to the door, Grayson in the lead. His deep frown told me he was growing more frustrated by the minute.

Before closing the door, Cody peered back at me over his shoulder. "See you soon, beautiful."

CHAPTER TWELVE

EMBER

As soon as they were gone, I headed for the shower. While I wanted to investigate every square inch of the house, the smell of dirt and dried blood overpowered my desire to snoop.

I was thankful, though. Had I woken up washed and in different clothing, I would've lost my mind. There were some things no one should ever do, and touching a person when they were at their most vulnerable—sound asleep—was one of the worst.

I made my way into a bathroom I could only describe as unbelievable. I'd watched my share of *Cribs* back in the day, but this room rivaled even the most impressive ones I'd seen.

An oversized bathtub stood in the center of the room. And in case someone wasn't in the mood to soak, there was also a gigantic shower in the opposite corner. Shelves filled with all types of candles, soaps, various toiletries, and stacks of towels lined one wall.

And hanging above all this unbelievable goodness were two giant chandeliers. It was over-the-top.

I locked the door and then quickly undressed, anxious to get under the hot water. The clothes I'd been wearing weren't much more than rags at this point. As I stared at the pile of fabric on the tiled floor, I thought about all I'd been through in such a short time. I'd been so caught up in the events of the day, I hadn't given myself time to process everything.

A magical creature had tried to kill me, and these men were telling me I was a wolf, or more accurately, *half* a wolf.

Yet, that couldn't possibly be true. Could it?

Another thought hit me as I wavered on my feet.

I was no longer as afraid as I was when I'd awoken in this realm a short time ago. Somehow, I felt I would be okay—that I didn't have to run. That they were serious about wanting to help me.

But I also had to admit as good as it felt, it also bothered me.

Because everyone always wanted something in exchange for helping you.

I made my way over to the large shower, turning the water on full blast. Nice and hot, just the way I liked it. As I stood beneath the cascading water, soaking my skin, my body began to relax.

What if?

I knew better than to play that game. What if-ing never got anyone anywhere. Still, I couldn't seem to help myself.

What if I was a wolf?

And then the most dangerous and unsettling *what if* of them all...

What if I was someone's fated mate?

It was almost impossible for me to think I could ever matter to someone that much. To be loved unconditionally, *forever.* And to love someone back just the same.

Sure, I couldn't deny the incredible attraction I felt when I was around them. I liked their attention and their touch more than I wanted to admit.

The way Cody had looked at me and how his lips had felt

against mine. How possessive they'd been, how insatiable. It was like he couldn't get enough of me. And I'd wanted him just as desperately. My fingers had ached to explore every inch of his muscular body, to know what he tasted like.

Grayson, however, was another story. I was deeply attracted to him physically, but he was more than a little rough around the edges. When he'd touched my cheek so softly, every part of my body had come alive, but he was an equal mix of quiet and thunder. Such a simple, gentle gesture had ignited *something*—though what it was, I couldn't say.

And Alex. In the small amount of time I'd spent with him, he'd made me feel safe. His energy was calm and soothing, as though life could throw him a deadly curveball, and he'd still hit a home run. I wasn't used to someone who carried such a peaceful sense of control about him, and I wanted to bathe my mind in that serenity, if only for a short time.

I felt so much—*too* much considering I barely knew them.

How was it possible?

I took a deep breath and leaned against the shower wall. It was probably just run-of-the-mill sexual attraction. I couldn't let myself get sidetracked by it. Learning more about this world and why I was attacked by the creature was all I needed to focus on.

It was more than enough to worry about.

As I soaped up, I thought about my history and what little I knew about it. Growing up an orphan, I had no idea which parent I took after or even who I looked like. Which also meant I had no one to thank or blame for my passions or problems in life.

And I'd always been okay with that. Or, at least, as okay as someone could be. I had at least come to terms with never knowing who my parents were, and so there was no point in asking questions no one had the answers to.

But suddenly, I wasn't so sure that was the case. If what they said was right, and I was part wolf, didn't that mean at least one of my parents had lived in *this* world?

I ignored the wings of hope fluttering in my chest. It was too soon to invest fuck-bucks in the idea that being in this strange place could somehow lead me to learning more about my family. I wasn't going to set myself up for heartache.

I stepped back under the water and let it pound against my shoulders as my thoughts returned to the three men who'd saved my life—men who believed that under the brilliant light of a fallen moon, I would learn to awaken my wolf.

Would the transformation happen?

The Fallen Moon was in a few days, which meant we'd find out soon enough.

I finished rinsing the soap from my hair, turned off the water, and stepped out of the shower as I wrapped myself up in an oversized towel. My mind was just as tangled as my hair. As I searched for a comb, my reflection made me pause.

What was that flicker in my eyes?

Was that hope?

Ignoring it, I found what I was looking for, combed through my hair, and then headed back to my room to search for clothing. All I needed was a t-shirt and a pair of jeans, and I'd be good to go.

Grayson had told me Cody had purchased some things for me, but I wasn't prepared for what I discovered when I began exploring the massive closet.

No, *closet* didn't come close to describing just how enormous the room was. It was bigger than my apartment.

Opening drawers, I found stacks of soft, cashmere blouses in every imaginable color, along with a wide variety of jeans, skirts, t-shirts, and even boxes of shoes, all carefully placed on the many shelves and tables throughout the massive space.

I opened the next door to discover an assortment of dresses. Some with sequins, others more casual summer dresses. While still dozens of other hangers contained cocktail dresses and even gloriously detailed evening gowns.

He'd purchased more for me than I'd ever owned in my entire life.

More than I could've ever hoped to own.

If I'd felt out of my element before, I certainly felt like I'd stepped into a different world now.

No pun intended.

I wasn't even sure what shoes went with what.

Suddenly, the little girl in me was delighted by the idea of playing dress-up, but I knew I didn't have a lot of time before the guys came back.

Despite being out of my comfort zone, I bypassed the jeans and t-shirts, choosing a shimmering, red dress.

It was a simple slip-on that didn't require zipping up the back, nor did it have beads or lines of sequin. It was a good compromise. I'd be comfortable but still show Cody just how much I appreciated all he'd done for me.

I slipped it over my head and shivered as the soft material pooled at my feet before I lifted the straps over my shoulders.

I was braless, having tossed mine into the trash, but the dress was low enough in the back I couldn't have worn one anyway.

A smile lifted my lips at the thought that as much as Cody had purchased for me, he'd skipped the lingerie section. I couldn't say I blamed him. Having to figure out my own bra size was a challenge at times, much less a guy trying to work it out.

But to my surprise, I realized how wrong I was when I opened the last door of the closet and discovered the shelves were filled with panties, stockings, and even bras. I lifted one, eyeing the size and realized he'd been *really* generous with his estimate.

Laughing, I ran my fingers over the folded layers of panties he'd chosen for me. Everything from black and red lace to simple cotton in pastel colors. He must have purchased everything the shopkeeper had thrown his way.

I wondered what the women in the shops thought when the lead beta of the clan stormed in looking for women's lingerie. As awkward as I felt, the idea he'd handpicked all of this for me was more than a little sexy. And hotter yet that he clearly hadn't cared what anyone thought about it.

I slipped into a black pair of lace panties. The least I could do was wear one of the more daring pairs for him. Not that he'd see them. Courage, when it came to men, was something I'd always lacked. With a man as gorgeous as he was, I doubted I'd ever have the nerve.

But a girl could dream.

I walked over to the full-length mirror and surveyed myself.

I felt pretty.

I hadn't thought of myself this way in so long that I panicked, suddenly second-guessing whether the dress was the right choice.

Who was I trying to fool?

I slipped my hands over my hips and down the front of the gown, smoothing it out. The material was gorgeous, hugging me in all the right places. I'd never worn something so elegant— or so sexy— but it felt amazing.

"Breathe," I said to myself as I quickly made my way downstairs before I could change my mind like the chicken-shit I was.

When I neared the bottom of the stairs, I decided to explore a bit, find something to drink to take the edge off, and wait for them to return. But when I turned the corner, I came face to face with Cody and Alex who stared at me with fire in their eyes.

For a split second, I thought about turning around and running back up the stairs, but before I could move so much as a muscle, Cody stepped forward and placed his hands on my shoulders, gently trailing his fingers down my arms.

And despite knowing better, my heart returned to the dangerous game of *what if* I'd been trying hard to steer clear of.

What if my story was just beginning?

CHAPTER THIRTEEN

ALEX

When Ember emerged from the staircase, she took my breath away.

The desire to claim the beauty standing in front of us wearing a dress which highlighted every curve was almost too much to bear. The yearning only intensified with every step she took.

She looked so sexy, I nearly lost the ability to speak.

"Thank you for everything," she said to Cody, her voice barely above a whisper. Her eyes were downcast as though she was afraid of his reaction. It was like she'd never been told just how exquisite she was.

"You really need to stop thanking me." Cody chuckled. "The sight of you is all the thanks I need. You're stunning."

Her fingers trembled as she accepted his outstretched hand, and he helped her take the final few steps down the staircase.

"You have great taste," she murmured. "I've never owned anything like this before. It feels so...lovely."

My wolf wanted to howl as I watched them so close together. Then I felt the power of Cody's wolf match my own.

Jealousy was an ugly beast, and I had to remind my wolf that we had no reason to be so possessive. She wasn't ours, though my wolf seemed to think otherwise. It took all my effort to keep him from thrashing to the surface.

"I just wanted to make sure you had everything you needed," Cody told her, clearly ignoring the intensity of my wolf who was raging, though I knew he felt it. We always sensed each other's energy, especially when we were possessive about something.

And we seemed to be more than a little possessive about Ember. Which was odd for all of us when it came to a woman.

"And there are always so many events and parties, so I thought you could use a few things in case you..."

Cody paused, and when he finally turned to look at me, I knew why. He wanted her to stay, that much was clear. But he knew how Grayson felt about it and how our clan would feel, not to mention how Ember might feel about it. She barely knew us, didn't know her wolf, and had just discovered that a whole world of magic existed.

We all knew the situation for what it was.

She was here for a good time, not a long time.

I pushed the troubling thoughts from my mind when she smiled at me and stepped forward. Her scent was intoxicating, a blend of honey and lavender.

"In case I what?"

I forced a smile though I didn't quite feel it. "In case you decide to stay."

The expression on her face became unreadable.

I cleared my throat and turned my attention to the window. "Do you want me to show you around? Maybe go for a walk, get some fresh air while these guys cook dinner?"

"Sure," she replied. "I'd love that."

I couldn't help but notice how Cody's jaw clenched and his body stiffened, but I didn't care. I wanted to get to know Ember better. Besides, she looked like she could use some fresh air.

"What's this about dinner?" Grayson asked as he made his way into the room. "Liza's gone till tomorrow, and I'm starving."

He stopped in his tracks when his gaze locked on Ember, and for a split second, I was sure he was about to charge forward and yank her into his arms, but to my relief he didn't.

"I thought maybe you or Cody could throw something together," I replied. "Ember and I are going out for a walk." Cody's mouth dipped down in a frown, but he didn't say anything.

"Since when does Cody cook? Do you want her to be back in bed, this time with food poisoning?"

"Ignore him," Cody replied with a smirk. "How do you like your steak, Ember? We make a mean one."

Grayson narrowed his eyes. "What he meant to say is *I* make a mean one while he sits and watches."

Ember laughed, a sweet sound that tripped up my heartbeat. "Medium well would be great. And thank you."

Grayson nodded wordlessly, his stare still trained on Ember's figure. I watched him take her in, transfixed by her beauty. I'd seen him look at many women before—and bring even more women home for the night—but I'd never seen him look at anyone *that* way.

"Give us thirty minutes, and it'll be ready." Grayson finally tore his gaze from Ember long enough to shoot Cody a look that said he wasn't getting off so easy this time. "And you're helping. It's about time you learn to cook and not always rely on Liza to do it for you."

I wanted to laugh at that. He was a good one to talk. Grayson and I both relied on our chef for all our meals. The only time either of us ever cooked was when she was on vacation, like now. Otherwise, there was no way Grayson would be behind a grill.

"Teach me your culinary ways, oh, Master Chef." Cody smirked before winking at Ember.

Grayson grumbled something incoherent as he and Cody disappeared through the door, headed toward the kitchen. I laughed at the expression on Ember's face.

"Are they always that way?"

"When it's just us, yes. Pretty much all the time. They fight like brothers." I chuckled. "But they'd also put their lives on the line for each other. So, don't let their banter fool you."

Her eyes gleamed with amusement. "They're hilarious."

I smiled at the idea that in just a couple days, if we were right, we'd meet her wolf. And somehow, I knew everything would start to make sense. Then maybe she'd stop questioning herself...and us.

We headed toward the foyer, my hand still holding hers and her sweet scent making my body ache with desire. But my mind settled on something else, and it filled me with dread.

What if all three of us wanted to claim her?

What would that mean for our friendship? For our clan?

Her wolf stirred when I squeezed her hand a bit tighter. Her beast wanted out, and I knew whenever she surfaced, she would be glorious.

CHAPTER FOURTEEN

EMBER

A lex and I made our way through a series of rooms until we were stepping into a giant foyer. It was impressively decorated in earthy tones giving it an elegant yet cozy look. As we neared the front door, I spotted a large table with a beautiful glass vase filled with white lilies in the center.

Whichever bachelor owned this house, he had exquisite taste.

"Lilies were my mom's favorite flower," Alex said, answering my question and making it clear he'd noticed me staring at the massive bouquet. "I like to keep a vase filled with them."

I smiled at the sweet gesture. I wanted to ask him more about her but thought twice about it. From the look on his face, it was clear he missed her dearly, and I didn't want to spoil his mood.

"So, you all live here?"

"No, just me and Grayson." He guided me around a corner to the entrance. "This place is big enough for the two of us, that's for sure. We each have our own wing." He leaned closer to me as if he was about to share a secret. "I still get lost sometimes."

I laughed as we made our way toward the front doors.

"It's a little chilly at night. Let me grab you a coat. I'm pretty sure Cody bought you one."

Within seconds, he was draping a long, white coat over my shoulders. It was as soft as butter with large buttons and a beautifully trimmed hood.

Once outside, I breathed in the cool night air and peered around the expansive property which was beautifully lit up with soft, white lights.

There was a row of large houses to the right of where we stood, as well as what looked like smaller cottages scattered off in the distance, dwarfed by Alex and Grayson's massive estate. If the size of someone's house meant anything, it was clear the Alphas were the most important and powerful of them all.

"We'll just take a short walk," he said, his hand still holding mine. "I know you're tired, and dinner will be ready soon."

"Sounds great."

We strolled down a cobblestone walkway as he talked about the different families who lived in the area. I could tell from the tone of his voice that his clan was more than just a settlement or village of people. They were his family, and the more we chatted, the more I realized just how much his pack meant to him.

"I never expected to be made Alpha," he said as we made our way across the property, cutting through what looked like an apple orchard. "My older brother was next in line. Not me."

"Did your brother not want to lead?"

As soon as the question was out of my mouth, I regretted asking it. The expression on Alex's face told me this was a painful conversation to have, yet he pushed forward.

"Our father believed in the old ways, including choosing who his son married. He said he wanted to keep our clan strong, and in his mind, that meant forming alliances with other leaders. He wanted Jackson to mate with the daughter of the Sable Crest clan."

"And he didn't want to?"

He shook his head. "He outright refused, and when it came to our father, refusing to take orders was something you just didn't do. He threatened to banish Jackson from the clan if he didn't agree. Then one day, my brother was gone."

"So, your father made him leave?"

Alex shrugged. "My father swore to me he didn't. He said he'd arranged for the Sable Crest Alpha and his daughter to visit that week so they could solidify the arrangement, but when the day came, Jackson was nowhere to be found." Alex let out a deep sigh. "My brother and I were close. I would've never thought he'd leave without telling me. I wish I knew where he was so I could bring him home. Let him take his rightful place in the clan."

"Maybe he'll come back soon," I replied quietly. "Now that your father isn't Alpha, and he wouldn't be forced to mate with someone he didn't love."

I was always so awkward with conversations like this, never knowing what to say.

The girl who blurted out all the wrong things at a funeral?

Yeah, that would be yours truly.

Alex shrugged. "It's been quite some time now. I just hope he's happy. Wherever he is."

He slowed his pace, and I was thankful for it. I could barely keep up with his long legs.

"When my father died, I became Alpha. And the first thing Grayson and I did was put an end to all that. No arranged marriages or forcing people to do anything else they don't want to do."

"I'm sure your clan was very happy you did that. I can't imagine being forced to marry someone I didn't love... So, how long have you known Grayson and Cody?"

Alex smiled, and I was relieved to see his expression lighten. "All our lives. As you know, Grayson and I share the role of Alpha. And Cody, he's our beta and a close friend."

We abruptly stopped, and I looked up to find we were standing in front of a large, stone building. It seemed to be more of a castle than any ordinary house, and I couldn't stop myself from admiring its opulence.

"This is Cody's house. Or rather, domain." Alex chuckled as though reading my mind. "His mom used to live here with him, but she passed away last year. All he has left is us."

I thought about the day when I first met Cody at the carnival and what he'd said to me. "What about Trinity?"

Alex turned to look at me briefly, clearly surprised by my question.

"He mentioned having a sister when we first met."

"Right. Yeah, she's been gone for some time now." His voice was full of sadness, and I realized I'd hit on yet another touchy subject. "She liked to travel and explore on her own, even though Cody always insisted on her taking someone with her. She left around the same time Jackson did and hasn't made it back home."

My heart suddenly felt heavy. Both Alex and Cody had lost someone they loved. Mysteriously disappeared without a trace. The thought made me nervous.

Did people get so easily lost in this world, unable to find their way back?

Suddenly the world seemed so imposing, so frightening, and I wished I could go back to a time, not long ago, when I naively believed the only world that existed was the one I lived in. I felt so selfish, having lived in self-pity for years, thinking everyone had it so much better—so much easier—than I did. Now, thinking about Alex's brother and Cody's sister, both lost and unable to come home, or worse, suddenly made my problems seem so small.

Cody's words echoed in my ears. *You can leave if you want to.*

I peeked at Alex and met his sorrowful expression. "So, you guys don't have any idea where Trinity might be?"

He shook his head. "Cody looked for her every day. He still goes out searching. He spent so much of the last few years venturing into different areas of the realm, even ones that are very dangerous to shifters. But nothing." He nudged me gently with his elbow. "He did the same for you."

"Me?"

"Yeah. Cody wouldn't give up on the idea his mate was out there somewhere, though you'll never hear him admit that in front of Grayson. But between searching for you and Trinity, he hasn't been home much. I've seen the way Cody looks at you. He believes you're meant to be his. There's no doubt about that." He paused a moment, his steps slowing. "We're close to a portal," he said, his voice growing quiet. "When I was younger, I'd get so lost in my thoughts that I'd end up walking straight through one without realizing it."

"This world of yours," I replied. "Full of magic, portals... it's pretty amazing." I wanted to say more, especially about Cody, but I didn't know where to begin.

"It sure is."

The thought of Cody spending so much time desperately looking for his family and his mate hit me harder than I could've expected. Seeds of sadness blossomed in my chest. But we barely knew each other. I wasn't sure how he could be so sure *I* was meant to be his mate.

"So, what about Grayson?" I asked, curious to learn more about the man who could go from ice to fire in seconds. "He doesn't seem too happy that I'm here, and I don't want to cause any problems."

"Grayson," Alex murmured as though saying his name alone was exhausting. "He's a good friend. Very loyal. And believe it or not, he's a Mama's boy. Visits her every week and makes sure she's taken care of. He even hired a full team to cook and clean for her. Just don't tell him I ever said that." He chuckled. "But he's also quite complicated."

"How so?"

"His family are the original settlers. They created our clan, so he's very loyal to our kind. Struggles with anything that isn't a wolf."

I cocked an eyebrow. "So I take it humans and halflings aren't exactly on his Christmas card list."

Alex chuckled. "He'll come around. It'll just take him some time. He's been through a lot."

I wanted to press him for more information, but I got the sense he was being careful with what he told me, and quite frankly, it wasn't my place to pry. Still, despite how heavy the conversation seemed with talk of loss everywhere we turned, somehow Alex made me feel comforted. Safe.

"How did you and Grayson both end up being an Alpha?"

"His father and mine led the clan together, so whether I had agreed to be Alpha or not, Grayson would've taken his father's position."

"And he's a good leader?"

"The best a clan could ask for. He will always put us first. Even before his own happiness." He slowed his step. "You ready to head back? They should have dinner ready by now."

"Not yet. The fresh air feels good. If you don't mind?"

We turned and ended up on another path, this one framed by rows of cherry trees, their long branches reaching out as if to welcome us.

"Not at all. I love being out here."

"I'm sure you do. Being a wolf and all that."

"Yes, and all that." He laughed. "You know, we can show you if you want. We could shift for you. If you don't think it'll frighten you. I wouldn't want to do anything that makes you uncomfortable, but maybe it'll help prepare you for when your wolf surfaces."

"It wouldn't scare me. But don't you have to, you know, get naked before you shift?" Heat spread over my cheeks.

He laughed. "We try to, yeah. If we don't, our clothes are pretty much destroyed. But don't worry about—"

"I'm not worried. But I'll wait until the Fallen Moon. It's only a few more days, after all." The truth was the thought frightened me. I wasn't so sure I was ready to watch three men turn into wolves right before my eyes, especially because they were sure I, too, would be turning into a wolf soon.

"Are you cold?" he asked. "You're shivering. Let's get you back to the house."

"No, I'm fine."

Clearly he'd noticed how I'd tightened the coat around me. It was a bit chilly, but I was enjoying the walk and being alone with Alex for the first time. I didn't want it to end so soon.

But as the sky darkened above us, it was clear Mother Nature didn't give a damn about what I wanted.

"Looks like a storm is on its way. It's been raining off and on for weeks now. It always happens right before the Fallen Moon. Come on, let's head back."

The trees swayed above our heads as the wind began to pick up. Yet, over the sound of rustling leaves, I heard my stomach growl.

"Supper will be ready soon, no worries."

I blushed, embarrassed by how loudly my hunger had betrayed me.

"And Grayson really does make one hell of a steak. When he actually cooks."

"It sounds so good right about now." I cocked my head to the side when a sudden thought popped into my head. "What kind of meat is it?"

"Beef, of course." He laughed. "We're not total savages."

CHAPTER FIFTEEN

CODY

"**G**rab an extra bottle!" Grayson shouted as I made my way down into the cellar, searching for his favorite brand.

They had crates of the stuff, though I wasn't usually in the mood to drink.

Tonight, however, I certainly felt like celebrating.

I found what I was looking for and carried the bottles back upstairs. "Brought up a Chardonnay as well. No idea what she likes."

I surveyed the dining room, impressed by the lavish feast Grayson had prepared. While we usually ate on our own, it was nice to be together like this, just like old times. Happier times.

"I'm sure she'll be fine with either," Grayson replied, setting the table with all the plates and cutlery we'd need.

The meal looked fit for a king, and I chuckled when I noticed he'd also lit the candles on the small tables in the corners of the room. I'd known him all my life, yet I never knew him to be the romantic type.

I uncorked a bottle of red and poured a little into two

glasses, handing him one. "Sit down and take a break. Everything looks great."

He fidgeted, then raked his fingers through his hair sheepishly as though he wanted to undo all he'd done. I didn't mean to call him out or embarrass him. It was just so out of character for him to go all out like this.

"Seriously, great job." I slapped him on the back playfully. "And I'm fucking starving."

"You aren't the only one."

We turned to find Alex making his way into the room with Ember trailing closely behind him. My cock stiffened when she got near, and I chastised myself internally. I had to learn to control myself. I couldn't afford to act like a horny teenager every time she was in my presence. But damn, she turned me on.

"It smells amazing," she murmured.

She shrugged out of her coat and laid it over her arm. "Where can I put this?"

"I'll hang that up for you." Grayson reached out and took it from her, disappearing from the room momentarily.

I almost laughed at the way Alex cocked an eyebrow over Grayson's unusual behavior.

I returned my attention to Ember, who was eyeing the platters of food like she couldn't wait to dig in.

"Tomorrow, you should spend some time in the shops. This week we have vendors from all over the realm setting up. Artisans, painters, jewelry makers... I'm not sure what you're into, but it could be fun. Just tell them to put whatever you want on our account," I said.

"This one," Grayson said, as he reappeared, gesturing at me, "spends more time shopping than he does helping with clan business."

"There's more to leading the clan than deciding what land we'll acquire next," Alex replied in my defense. "But that's a conversation for a different day." It was clear he wasn't in the mood to get into a pissing contest with Grayson.

"So, Cody, you're a doctor?" Ember asked.

"I am," I replied.

Obviously, she'd sensed the tension in the room and was doing her best to diffuse it. I appreciated it, and I knew Alex did too.

"Doctor Madden is a world-class obstetrician." Alex winked. "He's also somewhat of a local legend. At least that's what he'll tell you."

Ember laughed as I took a seat next to her.

"I'm sure he's great at his job." She turned to me. "You just seem so young to be a doctor. In my world, it takes years of medical school to accomplish that."

"Shifters learn at a much faster rate," I replied. "I'm honored to be able to help deliver pups. Feels like my calling, you know?"

Grayson picked up a platter of food. I wasn't kidding when I'd told him he'd done a great job. Plates of thick, juicy steaks as well as mounds of mashed potatoes, grilled asparagus, and all the fixings were passed around the table.

"Speaking of which," Alex asked as he refilled his glass. "Did Penny have her pups yet?"

I shook my head. "Not due for a couple of weeks, but she's counting the days. Twins aren't easy to carry around for four months."

"*Four* months?" Ember stopped spooning mashed potatoes onto her plate, her brow cocked. "Not nine months?"

Grayson gulped down his wine and shook his head. "You'll find we have very few things in common with your world."

"But the differences are what make things interesting," Alex added, trying to soften the bitter edge to Grayson's tone.

"I see," Ember replied. She took a bite of her steak and moaned. "Oh my God, this is so good."

I peeked at Grayson and could tell the sexy sound coming from her lips affected him just as much as it did me.

And there we were, reduced to horny teenagers once again.

"Now onto other important matters." I lifted Ember's empty glass. "White or red?"

Ember laughed. "Red, please."

A woman after my own heart.

"So, the night of the Fallen Moon," Alex said as he stuck a fork into a piece of meat and plopped it down onto his plate before passing the platter to Grayson. "We want you to know we'll be there with you through it all. No matter what happens."

"I was thinking about that," she replied. "You guys believe I'm only half a wolf because I haven't shifted before. But how can you be so sure?" She took a sip of her wine before continuing, "Maybe it just wasn't my time. Have you ever heard of someone taking longer to shift? I'm just not sure I understand what the difference is between a halfling, as you call it, and a full-blooded shifter."

Grayson gulped down his wine and shook his head as if her comment was the most foolish thing he'd ever heard. "There's a huge difference. For starters, we can shift whenever we want to. Apparently, that's not the case with you. And obviously, humans are much weaker, which means even if you do shift, your wolf might be rather useless."

His tone wasn't lost on me, and when he clenched his jaw, it was clear Alex had kicked him under the table.

I knew Grayson didn't mean to come across as such a jerk, but the last thing Ember needed to deal with was his passive-aggressive bullshit, especially only a few days before she'd discover whether her wolf would surface or not.

Sure, he had a reason to despise humans, but what had happened to him had nothing to do with her.

"What Grayson meant to say," Alex said, forcing a smile, before continuing, "is that there are likely many differences and some we aren't even aware of. The truth is, we've never met a half-shifter before, so we don't know what your limitations might be. But like I said, we'll be there if you need us. It's the least we can do."

Ember cocked her head to the side. "The least you can do? You saved my life. You brought me here so I could heal." She took another sip from her drink. "If anything, I owe you guys."

"You don't owe us anything, Ember," I replied. "One thing about shifters is that we look out for our own." I glared at Grayson, wanting to remind him that even if she was half-human, wolf blood still ran through her veins.

"No, some shifters only look out for themselves," Grayson replied sharply. Then he took a deep breath, and I could feel him trying his best to control his temper. "But at least *most* of us will always have each other's back. Unlike fucking vampires who wouldn't know loyalty if it staked them in the face."

"Fae are even worse," Alex added with a chuckle. "They'd sell their mother's life force if it got them ahead."

"Vampires and Fae…" Ember stopped eating, her fork frozen midway to her mouth, her brow cocked. "I still can't get over the fact this is real."

"Yeah, it's real," Grayson replied. "But if you're lucky, you'll never meet any of them. Stick with us shifters."

I wanted to smile because all it took was a little talk of loyalty to get Grayson back on the same page. Ember's wolf may not have appeared to her yet, but there was no doubt she was there, rumbling beneath the surface. We just had to help her come forward.

"That's what I was trying to say, Ember," Alex added. "When I said it's the least we can do…what I meant is you've been on your own for so long, without a clan or anyone helping you connect with your wolf. It was wrong that you were left alone. Half a wolf or not, you're still one of us."

"We need to figure out what clan she belongs to," I added.

"We should stop by the Hunters' Lodge tomorrow. There are always a lot of elders there, and maybe one of them would know something. You never know, maybe we'll find out she belongs to ours."

"She doesn't," Grayson replied even though there was no way he could possibly know that. "You do realize our clan isn't going to accept her. Not unless she shifts, and even then, they won't be happy she isn't a full-blood."

Ember speared a stalk of asparagus so hard it nearly flew off her plate. "Would you guys stop talking about me as though I'm not here?" She turned her attention to Grayson, her brow furrowed. "Your clan wouldn't want me here if I don't shift soon?"

I wanted to snarl at him for throwing that out there, especially when it just wasn't necessary. Whether the clan wanted to accept her or not, should she decide to stay, they'd just have to get used to it. Especially if I convinced Alex and Grayson to accept her as mine.

Because regardless of whether members of our pack liked it or not, what the Alpha said went.

And in this case, two Alphas were eyeing her in a way that told me they wanted her to stay, whether they were ready to admit it or not.

"The clan will listen to what we say," Alex countered as though reading my mind, and I wanted to pat him on the back for speaking up. "They trust us, so they'll come around. And I honestly feel like it isn't going to be an issue." He peered at Ember, his gaze intense. "You're going to shift."

"About that," Ember said as I filled her glass again, then topped up my own. "Can you tell me a little more about this Fallen Moon?"

"Remember how I said it's when the moon is at its closest point to Earth?" I replied. "It makes us stronger than ever. It's a whole other level of enlightenment, you could say."

"And for many of our elders, if they've been weakened due to illness, they can be healed under the light of a Fallen Moon," Alex added. "But it only happens once every decade. That's why it's such a special night for our kind. In fact, none of us were old enough to be present for the ceremony before now. Only adult shifters participate."

"Why is that?" Ember asked before taking another bite of her steak.

"Younger shifters may not be able to handle the pull of a Fallen Moon. It can take years for us to gain complete control over our shifts, so we don't take any chances."

"Well, I'm excited. I don't know if I believe a wolf is living inside of me yet or not, but to be honest, I'm starting to hope there is."

Her statement meant so much, and when I glanced around the table, it was easy to see the others felt the same way. Even Grayson, who'd been quiet for the last several minutes, looked like he was relieved to hear her say that.

"I've heard the Fallen Moon can have other effects as well. Especially on Alphas," he murmured through a smirk. "If he has a she-wolf who can handle it, that is."

"So, tell us about yourself," Alex said, clearly ignoring Grayson, but Ember looked as though she wanted him to elaborate, though she eventually tore her gaze from his. "We want to know everything."

She chewed her food thoughtfully, then took a drink of wine. "I'm not sure where to start. My life has been pretty uneventful."

Alex's eyes crinkled as he smiled. "I doubt that. What about your family? Which one do you think is a shifter, and do you know why they wouldn't have told you?"

I couldn't help but notice the way Ember's fingers trembled as she lifted the glass to her lips. The question had clearly caught her off guard. I was about to change the subject when she cleared her throat.

"I wouldn't know." She set her glass down and folded her hands in front of her. "I was found on the steps of an abbey when I was just a baby. No one knew where I came from or who I belonged to." She tried to force a smile that never quite reached her eyes. "I was bounced from foster home to foster home until I turned sixteen. A couple of years earlier than I was legally allowed to be on my own, but they didn't care. I took a job at a carnival, and as they say, the rest is history."

We sat in stunned silence for a moment, none of us knowing what to say to everything she'd revealed. And even though every part of me wanted to console her, I got the sense it was the last thing she wanted.

And suddenly, so much began to make sense. Her wolf had never met family. Had never touched the magic of the generations before. It wasn't that her wolf was muted by choice. She'd simply never had a reason to awaken.

She'd never had a home.

A clan was more than a family to our kind. A clan was where our souls found peace and our spirits found strength. Without knowing one's clan, a shifter would always feel as though a part of themselves was missing.

"Would you know where to start looking for them? If you wanted to." Alex asked quietly as though he was weighing the words out on his tongue.

Ember's gaze met his for a long time. For a second, I wondered if we'd tread too far. The last thing I wanted was to see sorrow in her eyes.

Then, she made herself busy cutting a piece of her steak and dipping it into the peppercorn sauce. "If they wanted to know me, they wouldn't have left me like they did. I don't want to know people like that."

Alex and I both sighed, but it was he who spoke first. "I'm sorry, Ember."

"Don't be. I turned out okay. Even if I am just a halfling." She winked at Grayson.

I suddenly saw a different side of her. She used humor, not just to lighten a mood but to hide behind like a fortress.

And I also knew from the way she fiddled around with the food on her plate that she'd lost her appetite. But her tight smile and the way she blinked to stop tears from falling told me she wanted no sympathy.

"Just a halfling is better than being a full-blood from any other race," Grayson quipped, and a smile finally cracked his lips, though whatever else he said after that was a mere whisper in the background of my tangled thoughts.

The house could've caught on fire, and I wouldn't have noticed.

Ember's energy was a mix of loneliness and strength, and it struck my heart so fiercely I thought I'd have to excuse myself before I lost control of my desire to comfort her.

We all knew what loneliness felt like, but the deep longing in her eyes told me more than words ever could. Unlike the rest of us, who'd known the love of a mother and the guidance of a father, as well as the kindness of true friendships, Ember had spent her life alone.

"Raise your glass!" Alex said, pulling my attention back to them. "Let's drink to friendship and a strong clan." His gaze shifted to Ember. "And to you."

"Cheers!"

We drank and chatted throughout the evening. Ember had many questions about our family, what it was like to grow up a shifter, and how it felt being in our true form. And we asked our share of questions as well, though we kept it light, asking her about life in the human world, what kind of things she liked to do, and her passions and dreams for the future.

I was surprised to discover she'd never left the area she grew up in.

"I always wanted to travel," she said. "But never had the opportunity, though I did stay in some of the neighboring towns when the carnival moved locations."

"Well, I'd say you can check travel off your bucket list, being in a completely different world and all," I replied, and she laughed.

By the time the sun was close to peeking above the horizon, we were all completely wiped out and more than a little drunk.

"I better get home. I have some things I need to do tomorrow," I said, yawning. Things I knew neither Grayson nor Alex would approve of. I only prayed it would lead me to answers that would help Ember.

"Like what?" Grayson asked. He glanced at Alex, who'd started to clear the table. "Do we have something planned I don't know about?"

"No," I replied quickly. "Just a few personal errands, not clan business."

Grayson and Alex exchanged a look, but I was relieved neither pressed me for details. Instead, Grayson poured another glass of wine as he watched Alex pick up the empty bottles and set them in the recycling bin. "You do realize we have house-keepers for that, right?"

"Unlike you, he was taught to clean up after himself," I replied.

The flippant chatter between them about who was raised better always went on forever. It was in jest, for the most part, and I knew I was responsible for starting it with my comment. But I wasn't in the mood for it tonight. I had too many other things on my mind. Namely the thought of leaving Ember here while I returned to my home. My wolf whined at the thought. He didn't like it any more than I did. Maybe I could just stay here. Or take her with me.

"I guess I'm going to head out now," I said, anxious to see how Ember would react.

Disappointment flickered in her eyes. "Will I see you tomorrow?" Ember asked hopefully as I stood up and got ready to go. "I thought maybe I could come by and we could hang out?"

A satisfied smile spread across my lips. "How about dinner?"

"That would be great," she replied. "See you around six?"

Grayson shot me a questioning look, but I ignored it. If Ember was meant to be my mate, then his approval wasn't needed. He knew, and I knew it.

I understood he had his reasons to be wary of what the clan would say about their beta possibly mating with a halfling, but I didn't give a damn about any of that.

Besides, it wasn't like Ember had even agreed. As far as I could tell, she was doing her best to focus on what was to come —awakening her wolf.

But in time, perhaps I could convince her to give me a chance.

Ember stood and closed the distance between us, wrapping her arms around my neck and gifting me with the sweetness of her scent.

"Goodnight," she murmured, her breath a whisper against my neck. "I had a great time. And I know you don't want to hear it again, but thanks for everything."

Then she finally stepped back, turned, and nearly walked into Alex, who was waiting to embrace her. The smile on his face made her giggle. He was clearly a little drunk.

"I think I need to get some sleep," he murmured as he wrapped his arms around her waist.

A prickle of wariness swept through me when he touched her that way, and I couldn't help but notice the way he held her just a little too long.

"Sleep well, Em."

Em? Now he was using nicknames for my *mate?*

"Hey, do you want me to grab you some water? You should probably drink some before you go to bed. Otherwise, you'll have a nasty hangover." Grayson didn't even wait for her response. He filled up a glass and handed it to her.

Since when did he care so much?

"Good thinking. Thanks." She reached out with her free arm, and he leaned in to give her a quick hug.

When he stepped back, I saw the look on his face. It was a look filled with hunger, as though he wanted to rip her clothes off and fuck her right on the spot.

Suddenly, I didn't want to leave her alone with them. I wanted to yank her into my arms and bring her home with me where she belonged.

Something had changed. It was as though a Molotov cocktail of tension and testosterone had invaded the room. This energy, a silent yet territorial exchange among men, only happened for one reason.

Now, I realized there was more to how they'd been acting. And it went beyond merely wanting to help a woman learn more about her wolf.

I should've seen it coming. The way Grayson had softened around her—as much as he could ever soften—spoke volumes about the way he felt. And Alex... he'd always been a lady's man with his penchant for flirting, but the way he talked to Ember wasn't how he spoke with others.

But she was meant to be *my* mate, I could feel it. And I would burn the world down before I'd ever give up on the idea that one day I would be able to make her mine.

I couldn't take my eyes off her as every little movement and idiosyncrasy came into frame. It was as though I saw her through a clearer lens, not just the raging hormones which had dominated my every thought since I'd first met her.

She was all I could see. All I *wanted* to see. And I noticed every minute detail. The way she covered her mouth when she thought she'd laughed a little too loudly, the way she raked her fingers through her hair, or swayed from side to side just a touch whenever someone asked her a question that made her nervous.

And as Alex draped an arm around her shoulder in a way that looked as though they'd known each other all their lives, I saw her smile.

A smile with the power to light up the heavens because it was genuine. It was real. And as I gazed at her, I saw my future standing in front of me.

In front of *us*.

I could tell she'd spent a lifetime guarding her heart. It would take special care and patience for her to trust us fully. But I could also see the more time she spent around us, the more comfortable she was getting.

She looked happy.

Could she feel a connection to Alex? To Grayson?

To me?

I heard the sweet melody of her laughter once again, and my heart jackknifed in my chest. This curvy beauty with the broken smile held the fate of three men in the palms of her hands, and she didn't even know it.

That was the real power of a woman.

A woman who could offer us the one thing we all so desperately wanted but were too proud to admit.

Throughout the ages, families and friendships were destroyed because of it.

Promises were broken, and wars waged, all in the name of it.

Love.

And when I tugged her back into my arms and brushed my lips slowly against hers in a goodnight kiss, I knew I would do all those things if it meant one day I could be with her.

CHAPTER SIXTEEN

EMBER

I woke up early, feeling as though I could conquer the world. I hadn't felt such a high in as long as I could remember.

I quickly showered and got dressed, this time choosing a simple pair of jeans and a light pink blouse, complete with a pair of flats. They were cute. But more importantly, they were comfortable, and considering there was a good chance I'd be doing a great deal of walking, comfort was essential.

After all, today's mission was a rather complicated one: Find someone who knew about halflings and who was willing to share that information with me, a total stranger.

I knew I could've asked the guys to help me. After all, they'd know who best to turn to.

But the truth was, I was more than a little frightened.

I didn't know what I'd uncover when I started digging into my past and opening doors that should probably be left closed. But I knew I had to get to the bottom of it, one way or another.

Fear of the unknown is real, amiright?

I wasn't looking for my parents, exactly, but if that information happened to fall into my lap, I'd deal with it the best way I could. They'd thrown me away like I was nothing more than trash. There could never be a reason—or excuse—good enough to justify that.

I did, however, want to learn more about this wolf who lived inside me. Being a halfling meant I had two very different identities, and they'd never met. The human me, the woman who lived a rather ordinary life, and then this whole other entity.

I had to admit, even though I was more than a little afraid, I was also excited to meet her. Though the idea of her brought up more to worry about.

What if she was feral? Dangerous? Deadly, even?

All three men had looked at me with such warmth and kindness that I didn't want anything to change their minds. Even Grayson seemed to be at least trying to go easier on me as the evening progressed yesterday. So, I wanted to do this on my own.

I brushed my hair, put it up into a ponytail, and then headed down the stairs.

At dinner, Cody had mentioned something about going to see the elders at a place called Hunters' Lodge, so that was what I'd look for. Surely the older generation would know something about halflings.

As I made my way downstairs, I was so deep in thought I nearly ran into a woman who was headed toward me, a heavy tray balanced in her hands.

"Oh my God, I'm so sorry!" I said as I swerved out of her way just in time. "I need to pay attention to where I'm going. Maybe looking up when I walk would be a good start." I was more than a little embarrassed.

"No worries, my dear," she replied as she turned to me, clearly unfazed by the fact I'd almost smashed into her. "Did you sleep well?"

"Yes, very well, thank you." I was about to ask for her name when she lifted the tray, holding it out to me.

"I'm Liza, the resident chef. He asked me to bring this to

your room so you could enjoy breakfast in bed. But since you're up, would you prefer it on the terrace? It's a beautiful day outside."

I looked at her in confusion, then lowered my eyes to the tray and found a plate stacked with golden pancakes, bacon, sausage, fresh fruit, toast, an assortment of jams, and a pitcher of orange juice.

"He? Who do you mean?"

I reached out and lifted the jug of orange juice from the tray, hoping to lighten the load a bit. But Liza stepped back as if her only goal in life was to make sure the food made it to its destination.

"Yes, Mister Cross. I must say, this is the first time he's ever done that." She flashed me a warm smile before adjusting the tray, causing the dishes to rattle against each other. "Where would you like me to take this?"

I set the orange juice back down and took the tray from her hands. "I'll just eat downstairs. Thank you so much. It all looks delicious."

"As you wish," she replied. She blessed me with another brilliant smile before turning away and heading down the hall. "If you need anything, please let me know." Then she was gone.

With a lightness in my heart, I resumed my trek down to the dining room. A smile played on my lips as I thought about how sweet it was for one of them to send up breakfast. It also dawned on me I didn't know either of their last names, and considering I'd been holed up in their house recovering for days, it seemed more than a little strange.

I looked around, but there was no sign of either of them. Perhaps whoever had sent breakfast to my room did so because they had clan business to attend to.

Alphas. They were leaders of the Thunder Cove clan with Cody by their side. The night before, I'd asked them what sort of things an Alpha did. Alex had simply smiled and said they were responsible for governing the clan, acquiring new territory, negotiating with other clans, and protecting their realm.

But Grayson's expression had been dark when he'd added that they needed to start *leading* the clan and not letting it lead them.

Something was bothering him, but what it was I couldn't know.

I had too many questions. Worse, it felt as though my brain was about to short circuit from everything that had already happened.

One thing at a time, Ember.

I gobbled down the food, not realizing just how hungry I was until I was nearly swallowing a pancake whole and guzzling down another glass of juice.

My appetite before coming here was next to nonexistent. Some days I'd eat nothing more than a piece of toast on my way out the door. *But now?* I couldn't seem to eat enough.

When I finished, I cleaned up after myself and headed out the front door.

Enough with the questions. It was time for answers.

I strolled down the sidewalk into what I assumed was the central part of town. Alex had given me a sense of direction during our walk last night, so I followed along, walking east and then crossing over to the other side when the road took a sharp left.

Eventually, I ended up in what looked like a business district —though it wasn't exactly a bustling city, more like a mid-sized town.

But unlike any place I'd ever been in the human world, this one was breathtaking.

The streetlights were trimmed in gold. A large archway hung over the entrance proudly proclaiming *Welcome to Thunder Cove*.

Shiny sports cars and jacked-up trucks drove by, but they didn't look like any models I recognized—not that I was an automotive expert or anything. I didn't even own a car. But I had expected things to be very different from what we had in the human world.

After all, one would assume a world of magic had to be light years ahead of anything humans could ever imagine.

So part of me was stunned to discover that as intriguing as the world around me was, I didn't get the sense it was all that superior with regard to technology. In fact, quite the opposite seemed true. So far, I hadn't seen a single phone of any kind, let alone a laptop or tablet. It was yet another stark contrast to the world I came from, where people were glued to their devices.

Beneath my feet, the roads looked just as they did back in my world. And the clothing worn by those who shared the road with me seemed no different from the fabrics we wore back home. Even the road signs were similar.

I continued along, on the lookout for any sign of what might be a Hunters' Lodge, but nothing caught my attention. I took it all in, the sights, sounds, and smells around me—all three of which led me to my favorite kind of places: a bakery, a cafe, and finally, a series of colorful chip wagons.

It was such a quaint and cozy little town, and I was having a great time meandering through the different sections. But the farther I went, the more stressed I became that I had no clue where to find Hunters' Lodge, much less if an elder would even be open to talking to me.

I rounded the corner of another string of stores—a deli and another coffee shop. I decided to grab a cappuccino while I pulled myself together and figured out what to do next.

I knew the easiest thing to do would be to just ask someone for directions, but I was worried word would quickly spread that a stranger was in town looking for elders. I wasn't sure how Grayson, Alex, or Cody would feel about me doing this on my own.

I looked over to see the barista quickly making her way over to me.

"You were supposed to wait to be seated."

"Pardon?"

She nodded to the sign at the front of the shop—the sign I hadn't noticed—but judging by the look on her face, she wasn't going to let it slide. "Says it right there."

I stood up, prepared to go back to the front and wait for her to instruct me where to sit, but she shook her head in annoyance before wiping down the table.

"It's fine. Just remember to wait next time. Sometimes only a few tables are open though it hasn't been as busy—"

She stopped what she was doing, the cleaning cloth suddenly forgotten, and looked at me as though she was trying to remember something.

I shifted in my seat uncomfortably. "I'm sorry. I didn't see the sign, but I'll remember next time."

Though if she kept gaping at me like I'd grown a second head, there wouldn't be a next time.

"Are you from around here?"

There it was, and though I should've known it was coming, I wasn't prepared for how to answer the question. Clearly, the clan was a tight-knit group, and their town was the kind of place where everyone knew each other. So, what should've been no big deal—a woman venturing into a coffee shop—had already raised questions.

"Are you sticking your nose where it doesn't belong again, Marissa? Don't think your boss would be too happy to hear you're harassing customers." The voice from behind me carried a killing-her-softly tone, a blend of silk and lethal injection. In other words, she wasn't to be trifled with, and from the frantic look on the barista's face, she was very much aware of that.

"I was just making small talk," she bit back before picking up the cleaning cloth. "What can I get you?"

"I'll just have a coff—"

"Forget this place," the stranger insisted, stepping out from behind me. "They wouldn't know how to make a proper cappuccino if their life depended on it. Come on. I'll show you where to go."

The woman was stunning, with long, wavy, blonde hair, full red lips, and a perfect nose. I was sure if she took off her sunglasses, she'd have amazing eyes too. Not to mention she was dressed to perfection in a beautifully fitted black dress and heels that matched her lips. She was the kind of woman I'd caught myself staring at in appreciation on TV.

I used to dream of being a woman like that. So perfectly put together.

But it was the air of confidence that turned heads. This woman looked like she belonged on the cover of either *Fashion Forward* or *Boss Babes*.

Or both.

"Ready to go? Seriously, don't waste your time here."

She headed toward the door, towing along what looked like the aftermath of an expensive shopping spree. I found myself following closely, even before I'd made the conscious decision to do so.

"Ember, right?"

I felt a wave of panic roll through my chest at the revelation she knew my name.

When I didn't answer, she cocked an eyebrow and took a step closer to me.

"Don't worry, your secret is safe with me. Though to be

honest, after your little run-in with Marissa, I think that ship has sailed."

She adjusted the dozen or so shopping bags in her hands, acknowledged a woman who walked by, and then returned her attention to me.

"Relax. The clan can gossip all they want, but in the end, it really doesn't matter."

"Excuse me?"

"You being a halfling." She attempted to lift a hand to wave off any concerns I had, but the bags were apparently far too heavy. "Hey, can you do me a favor and take a few of these?"

I barely had time to react before she was shoving parcels at me. When she finally had a free hand, she reached up and pulled her sunglasses off, folding them and sticking them into her purse.

I was right; she had killer eyes—the color of the envy I was sure most women felt when in her presence.

"I'll say one thing," she continued, taking a few steps ahead until I got the hint I was supposed to catch up. "You're sure going to get those hens clucking. It's been quite some time since they had something new to talk about. And nothing ever so deliciously scandalous."

I remained silent, clueless about what to say or do, but when she stopped walking and turned to face me, her smile was as warm as a summer's day, and I could tell she meant no harm.

"Sorry, I'm such an asshole. Didn't even introduce myself." She offered a perfectly manicured hand, and I accepted. "I'm Selena Parsons. Cody told me all about you. In fact, he can't stop talking about you. Anyway, I swung by to say hi, but Alex said you were out. Figured you'd be down here."

I nodded and tried to get my mouth to start functioning before she thought something was wrong with me.

"You're friends with Cody?"

I could've asked her a hundred other things but knowing

what her relationship was with him somehow seemed the most important.

"We're family," she replied.

I breathed a sigh of relief.

"He's my cousin."

She zeroed in on a shop a few yards away and led me to it. We entered through a gate as she signaled to a server that we were claiming an outside table.

"The weather is too nice to sit indoors," she said as she plopped her bags down and relieved me of the ones I'd been holding. "And it's too damn hot to be drinking cappuccino," she added. "I say we go for something much cooler... and stronger." She winked at me, and I laughed.

"Can't go wrong with margaritas."

"Girl," she replied as a handsome young man came to our table. "I like how you think."

"You ladies need a menu?"

"We're good. Two margaritas, please."

He was gone for only a few minutes before he returned with our drinks. "Enjoy."

I didn't miss the way the man's gaze lingered on Selena as though he was waiting for her to take notice. When she didn't, he moved on to the next table, though I caught him glancing over every chance he got.

"That dude's got it bad."

She cocked an eyebrow in confusion, but then it registered. "Oh, Logan?" She rolled her eyes and took a sip of her drink. "He likes anything with a pulse."

I doubted that was true, but she seemed oblivious to just how captivating she was. It made it so easy to like her.

"But enough about Logan... or Marissa... or any of those ridiculous people. I want to know about you."

I stared at her, wondering how much I could trust her. I didn't have a great history with female friends. Growing up in foster care, we quickly learned it was every boy and girl for themselves. And even though I was an adult now, those lessons were hard to forget.

But she said she was Cody's cousin, and my instincts, though not always reliable, said she was someone I could trust.

"Cody is crazy about you," she replied. "Head over freaking heels."

Embarrassed, my gaze slipped down to the table.

How could that be true?

I'd spent such a short amount of time with him. Sure, Cody had kissed me—and I'd kissed him back—but it had to be purely physical. We barely knew each other.

"He's never let himself even get near the *L-word*." She took a sip of her margarita, then smiled at me as though I was her closest friend. "But I swear, he's madly in love with you."

"The L-word?" I shook my head. "No, no. That's impossible. Really. He's just helping me figure out where the hell I came from and whether this wolf of mine can ever surface. We don't know much about each other."

She surveyed me as though she was about to call my bluff but then thought twice about it.

"Well, he seems to believe there's something special about you, Ember. Us shifters, we're all about energy. We feel drawn to people in a way humans probably would never understand. There's either a connection, or there isn't. And when there is…" She whistled softly. "It's unbreakable."

"I don't know about—"

"Right, you don't know what clan you belong to and how that might affect things." She reached out and placed her hand on mine. "Don't worry. I think I know someone who can help with that."

I opened my mouth, ready to tell her that wasn't what I was going to say, but she must have read the expression on my face.

"Oh, were you going to say something about how there's no

connection between you and Cody?" She squinted her eyes at me as if she didn't believe a word I said, though I'd barely said anything.

"You know what? You're probably right. You don't feel anything for him. Not a thing." She sighed. "That's why you looked like you were about to scratch my eyes out when I first mentioned knowing him. And why you can't stop smiling when his name is mentioned." Her lips formed into a dramatic smile to emphasize her point. "You look like a fucking Cheshire cat when I say his name."

I laughed, and so did she.

"I get your point."

"Good," she replied. "Now, drink up. The old bastard tends to get into the moonshine rather early these days, but if anyone in this clan knows a thing or two about halflings, it's him."

This woman seemed to genuinely want to help me, and for some reason, I believed her. There was no judgment, no malice hidden behind a false smile.

"Thank you." I swallowed back the rest of my margarita. "For saving me from a bad cappuccino and wanting to help me figure out where the hell I came from. I appreciate it."

"All in a day's work," she replied before leaning across the table. "Just don't spread the word about the terrible cappuccinos. I don't have the heart to tell him, but the place has gone to shit."

"Tell who?"

"My dad." She snorted. "He owns the place."

I laughed.

CHAPTER SEVENTEEN

EMBER

To my surprise, Hunters' Lodge wasn't our destination. When I'd mentioned it, Selena shook her head and insisted she knew an elder who'd help us and that he'd also be discreet.

The man lived on the opposite side of town, but Selena dropped her shopping bags off at her dad's café and then called a taxi. Within minutes, we were headed down a long, dirt road that seemed to stretch on for miles.

During the drive, Selena asked me about my wolf.

"I can feel her energy," she told me as the driver peered at us through the rearview mirror for probably the tenth time since we'd climbed into the backseat of his car. "I'm surprised she hasn't emerged yet, but I guess it's a good thing, considering you wouldn't have known what to do."

I nodded. "When that creature attacked me, I didn't think I was going to survive."

Selena pursed her lips, and it was clear she was deep in thought. "I don't know much about the human world. I've never been there and never plan to." She raked her fingers through her silky hair and sighed. "I love being in my wolf form more than my human one. I'd let her surface all day if I could."

"Why can't you?" I asked.

She paused, and for a minute, I wondered if maybe I'd asked a taboo question, but then she leaned back against the seat and let out a deep sigh. "The clan worries about a subconscious split. That's where we'd become so disconnected from our wolf that we wouldn't remember the harm we might have done." She smiled, and it took the edge off her words. "So, we're only allowed to shift under a full moon, unless you're an Alpha or a beta, of course. Or any of the military or shifters in training. They can shift whenever they want."

"So, you feel more comfortable as a wolf?"

She nodded. "Very much so. But my wolf requires a lot more energy. Being in our human form helps our wolves rest, so I guess the forefathers knew what they were talking about. As much as I wish differently."

I thought about how I'd seen wolves outside of my window the morning I woke up in this world and how Cody had shifted back shortly before he'd first kissed me.

"Maybe Grayson or Alex will change the rules and allow you to shift even when it's not a full moon."

"Not a chance. The two of them idolized their fathers. Whatever rules were set by them will stay. Well, maybe, except one."

"Which one is that?"

The smile on her lips was nothing short of devilish. "Every member of our pack has only mated with full-blooded shifters so far. But I think Cody would break that rule if you'd let him."

A lump formed in the back of my throat, which I quickly swallowed down. The idea that Cody would go against the rules of his clan for me seemed more than a little risky, and I struggled to understand why he would put so much on the line for someone he barely knew.

But despite myself, I trembled with desire at the thought of getting to spend time with him later that night.

"I like him," I replied. "But like I said before, we hardly know each other."

She shrugged, all smiles. "Either way, if you wanted to be with him, I don't think it would matter if our Alphas approved or not."

"And you think this elder will be able to tell me what clan I belong to?"

It suddenly made sense, Selena going out of her way to help me find out who my clan was. She was Cody's cousin, and she believed he felt something for me... something that could cause chaos amongst the pack if things turned sideways. Helping me figure out my origins was her way of protecting him.

A thought suddenly formed.

"What if I'm from an enemy clan?" I thought about how Grayson had talked about battles over territory and how they'd lost so many loved ones. *What if whichever parent of mine was a shifter belonged to a rival? Would that bring war to their doorstep?*

I didn't miss the way Selena dropped her head so I couldn't see her expression. Suddenly, where I came from seemed so much more important than it ever had before.

Because in a world where your clan was the one thing that defined who you were, they couldn't easily accept me without knowing my origin.

And suddenly, *that* mattered more to me than I wanted to admit.

I felt at home in this world of magic. It was as though I'd been living a lie all my life and had finally discovered the truth. My wolf hadn't even surfaced yet. I wasn't ready to leave. Not yet.

"It'll be fine," Selena finally replied as she reached out and patted my knee. "Have faith."

A few minutes later, we pulled up to what could only be described as a ramshackle hut on the outskirts of town.

The cab driver glanced at us, his expression filled with concern. "Are you ladies sure you want me to leave you here? I can wait and bring you back when you're ready."

"It may take some time," Selena replied as she opened the door. "We'll be fine, but thanks."

I slid out of the car and followed her down the rocky driveway up to the rundown shack. Selena didn't seem at all fazed by how dreadful it looked, but as we stepped to the front door, she turned to me with eyes filled with warning.

"Let me do the talking, okay? Elders can get skittish around strangers, especially this one. Just relax and don't talk unless he asks you something directly."

I nodded while she leaned forward and knocked.

"Hold your horses!" a thin voice rattled from behind the door. "I'm coming!"

A few seconds later, the door was heaved open, and we found ourselves standing in front of a man so tall I wondered how he managed to not bang his head on the ceiling when he walked around his house.

"What do you want?"

Selena cocked an eyebrow. "Is that any way to greet your great-niece? I need your help."

The man's gaze clicked over to me as he assessed whether to slam the door in our faces or let us in. "And who's this?"

Selena stepped forward, and I could tell her patience was running thin. "That's what we're hoping to find out. Let us in, Elgin. We don't have all day."

I wanted to laugh at the way Elgin twitched his nose as though he couldn't stand the sight of us, but he stepped aside to let us into his home.

The interior wasn't much better than the outside. Selena led me to a worn-out sofa, and we sat next to each other while Elgin took a seat on the other side of the room.

He glared at me with suspicion, making it clear he wanted to keep his distance.

"My friend here was attacked in the human world," she began, her expression somber. "We don't know why, but Cody and the Alphas claim it was a wolf slayer."

"A lupus interfectorem in the human world?" he asked as he tilted forward.

Clearly, we'd gotten his attention.

"I've never heard of such a thing. They belong in the shadow realm with all the other dark things we'll not speak about." He tugged at his chin, deep in thought. "Only a dark witch could call such a creature out of its realm."

"But why would a witch want to do that?" Selena asked. "Have you ever heard of a wolf being attacked like that in the human world?"

Elgin narrowed his gaze as it locked on me. "You're from the human world? But I can sense your wolf."

His words hit my heart like a freight train. Every single pound in my chest was intensifying until his words repeated, drowning it out.

He can sense my wolf.

So, it was true; I was a wolf. Somehow an elder who looked as though he'd lived a hundred lives telling me he'd felt my wolf made it a reality I could no longer ignore.

I was frozen to the spot as chills ran down my spine, and that thrumming returned. My mind raced through my history like I was flipping the pages of a photo book, desperately searching for a cinder–just a single spark that would ignite a blazing fire of memories of my wolf.

But I found nothing.

"Yes," I finally replied. "I've been in the human world all my life. Or, at least for as long as I can remember."

"And yet you were able to enter our portal." His mouth twisted into a frown.

"Yes." I fidgeted under his scrutiny. "Cody and your Alphas saved my life. When I was attacked... they killed the creature and then brought me here so I could heal."

His eyes widened at my words, his expression grim. "They killed the lupus interfectorem?"

"They did."

Instantly, he was on his feet and headed to the far end of the room. "No...no, they shouldn't have done that."

He paused at one of the shelves, his boney fingers running over a series of books until he found what he was looking for. He pulled it from its place, flipped through the pages, and then stopped, reading intently, as though the page held the answers to all the questions of the universe.

"Did this creature mark you?" He glared at me with distrust.

"Did it *mark* me? I'm sorry, I don't understand."

"Did it claim your breath? When it attacked you, did it get close enough to steal your breath?"

I shivered as I thought about that night and how I was sure I was going to die when the creature stood over me. And how I'd felt a strange breeze as though it was—

"Yes," I replied. "It stood over me... I thought it was going to kill me, but it didn't. It was toying with me, sniffing me, breathing me in."

Elgin's mouth widened in horror. "Stand up and turn around."

"What?"

He took a tentative step toward me as though the creature might burst through my skin and attack if he got too close.

"Show me the back of your neck."

"Elgin? What's going on?" Selena asked in a voice, mirroring my confusion. And my fear.

I held my breath as terror rushed through me, but I stood up and spun around as Elgin took a few more steps in my direction. "Lift your hair. I need to see the base of your neck."

I did as he instructed. His shuffling steps erased the distance between us. Selena stood and examined my neck, looking for some clue as to what Elgin was talking about.

"There!" Elgin screeched as he clambered back across the room. "You've been marked! It won't stop until it destroys you. And if it manages to invade this realm... it will destroy us all!"

"But, Elgin," Selena said, her voice trembling as she studied the mark on my neck. "They killed the wolf slayer. It can't come after her."

"No, *you* don't understand," Elgin replied as he lifted a finger and pointed at me. "The only reason she isn't already dead is because her wolf hasn't emerged. Once it does, the shadow realm will only send another to claim her. They already have a taste of her soul. They won't stop!"

He slid the book across the floor, and Selena picked it up with trembling fingers.

"Selena? What does it say?" I peered over her shoulder as she scanned the page, but when she lowered the book and turned to me, her expression said more than words ever could. My stomach dropped and my mouth went dry.

"I'm so sorry," she replied as a tear slipped from the corner of her eye. "He's right. There's a tiny mark on the back of your neck that matches this."

She lifted the book, and I stared at the paper—at the illustration of the creature who'd scorched my heart in terror and the outline of a thin, curved line.

My fingers flew to the back of my neck, but I couldn't feel anything. Selena had said it was small so it made sense that Cody, Grayson, and Alex hadn't noticed it.

I looked up at Selena as my heart hammered in my chest.

"Ember, that doesn't mean the creature can enter this realm. We'll find a way to make sure you stay safe."

My gaze returned to the page. Beneath the illustration was a passage, describing how once a lupus interfectorem was called, it would seek out its target until it had claimed the soul of a wolf.

Should the creature be destroyed, another would eventually appear in its place.

If that book was accurate, I'd be dead before my wolf had ever truly lived.

CHAPTER EIGHTEEN

EMBER

Selena and I sat in silence while the cab driver drove us back into town. When he dropped us off outside of Grayson and Alex's house, she finally spoke.

"We have to find more information before we tell anyone."

I furrowed my eyebrows in confusion. Surely we should let Grayson, Alex, and Cody know what we'd discovered so they could take me back to the human world before I brought danger to their clan. I would be putting their families at risk every day I was in their territory. I wouldn't blame them for wanting to get rid of me as quickly as possible.

Before I could respond, she hugged me tightly, and I realized I was wearing my emotions on my sleeve, despite trying hard not to.

"Ember, you're going to be okay. I promise."

When I started to explain why I felt it was important to speak to Grayson, Alex and Cody, she shushed me.

"We need a little more time. Once we know *all* the facts, we'll go to them. There's no point in doing that before we know everything. Please, trust me."

I nodded. I had no choice but to trust her.

After all, this was her clan, and she'd known the guys all her life. If she felt it best to keep this information to ourselves for the time being, there had to be a good reason.

"How do you think we can find out more? Elgin is an elder, but even he didn't offer up much after he discovered I'd been marked." I sighed. "After that, he couldn't get me out of his place fast enough."

"Elgin can be a bit over-the-top. Don't let his theatrics get to you." She waved a hand as if she was swatting a fly. "If wolf slayers could enter this realm, they would've by now. So obviously, they can't come through our portal."

She had a point. The tome didn't have a lot of information, and the little we'd read hadn't mentioned anything about whether the creatures could move freely into other realms— there was only mention of the human world, which wasn't protected.

"I'm sorry Elgin wasn't any help in giving you any information about what clan you might belong to, though. Part of me wishes we'd never gone to see him. All it did was stress you out even more."

"I'm glad you brought me to him," I quickly replied. "I appreciate all of your help, Selena. Really, you've been amazing."

I felt terrible she'd spent so much of her day helping me only to feel defeated because we weren't successful. "So, what's the plan? What can I do?"

"In a few days, after the night of the Fallen Moon, we'll meet up and discuss what to do next. Sound good?"

"Yes. Thank you."

She reached out and squeezed my hand. "We'll keep digging until we know everything there is to know. Then we'll figure out what we need to do."

I thought about how Alex had mentioned he and Cody had already explored the archives when investigating the creature, but I didn't say anything about it to Selena.

Did they already know the danger I was putting them into? If so, why did they allow me to stay?

Selena's voice dragged me from my thoughts. "Tomorrow is the night of the super moon. I know it'll be hard, but I'm hoping you can push this out of your mind just for now so you can focus on that. Your wolf will need every bit of energy you have when she awakens for the first time."

The Fallen Moon.

Now that I believed I was a shifter, my whole heart wanted my wolf to come forward and introduce herself. I prayed the power of the moon would be what she needed to surface.

"Okay, you got it." She looked at me as though she wasn't so sure, and she was right.

How could I possibly forget about learning I was marked by a shadow monster?

But I would at least try to focus on giving my wolf her best possible chance to awaken.

"Hey, did they tell you what will happen? It'll be the first time many of us have experienced a fallen moon since being old enough to truly understand it. Only adults who are in control of their wolves are actually allowed out for it. So, I'm excited but nervous."

"They told me about that. They also said shifters feel stronger and that the elders can be healed, but not much more than that. Part of me thinks they were worried about freaking me out."

She smirked. "Or they don't know what to expect. Like I said, none of us were adults during the last Fallen Moon."

"What are you nervous about?"

She peered up at the sky as though she was daydreaming about something. "Some say shifters find their true mates on the night of a fallen moon. That the moon guides us." She shrugged. "Not that I want to be tied down to anyone."

The expression on her face told a different story.

"Then you should be excited, not nervous. Whoever your fated mate is, he's a lucky man." I couldn't help but smile when she tilted her head to the side thoughtfully then nodded in agreement.

"You're right. I'm just hoping he's not from this clan. Maybe I'll be matched with someone from one of the wealthier clans. Like Silver Creek. They're supposed to be the wealthiest clan in all the realms." She giggled. "And I do have expensive taste."

"I heard Grayson talking about Silver Creek yesterday. He said members of the pack were coming here for a meeting."

"Really?" She perked up. "Did he say when?"

"I think he said a few days after the Fallen Moon, but I can't remember anything else. I know he didn't seem happy about it."

"Grayson hates the Silver Creek clan, but no one knows why. They've always been a peaceful clan, and it seems to me they'd make a great ally. They've never even stepped foot into our territory without permission. I can't say the same for Grayson."

"What do you mean?"

"Grayson goes where Grayson wants. Clans have agreements in place. Based on respect, really. We're supposed to notify them whenever we're going to enter their territories and vice versa. It makes sense, you know? With so many previous Alphas waging war on other packs throughout the years and all."

I nodded.

"But Grayson used to visit the clan all the time, when his Dad was still alive. I think he was really close friends with some of their members. Then, for some reason, he stopped going, and then suddenly they were the enemy."

She sighed. "That's one thing I don't like about Alphas. They set down rules without feeling the need to explain why. Just seems unfair. But, if the Fallen Moon reveals my mate to me and he's from Silver Creek, there'll be nothing Grayson can do to stop it."

"Fated mates," I replied. "The connection is that strong, huh?"

"Undeniable. Some people don't want to believe it's even real. Mainly because in the past some have been fated to their enemies, which as you can imagine, would've caused a lot of problems. But I believe in it. And you should too."

I cocked an eyebrow. "And why is that?"

"Like I said, it's undeniable. If Cody is your fated, like he seems to believe you are, you'll both know."

The mention of Cody made my heart race.

"Speaking of Cody, I better get going. I told him I'd be at his place at six o'clock."

She glanced at her watch. "You've got an hour."

Then she shot me a mischievous smile. "Just long enough to shower and shave your legs."

I laughed.

She had a point. I may have the blood of a wolf running through my veins, but that didn't mean my legs had to look the part. At least not tonight.

CHAPTER NINETEEN

CODY

I made my way to the back of the library. What I was looking for wouldn't be out in plain sight. It would be safely stored away, out of reach from clan members.

I unlocked the door and entered the dark space, searching for the light switch. I'd been in this same room with Alex not too long ago when we'd first brought Ember into the realm. We'd searched endlessly for whatever information we could find about the creature who'd attacked her.

What we'd discovered was the stuff that nightmares were made of—a dark force who lived in the shadow realm, a place none of us knew much about, just enough to stay away.

But I knew there had to be more information in one of the books—something Alex and I had overlooked.

I pulled one of the golden spined tomes off the shelf and thumbed through it quickly, my eyes peeled for any mention of the creature, but I came up short.

I thought about the night we'd fought the beast. It was vicious, pure evil incarnate. But when Grayson had lunged at it, rather than withdrawing, it had stayed close, its inky body winding through the shadows until we'd destroyed it.

It had taken all three of us, though I had no doubt it could have easily destroyed us all if it wanted to.

And that was what had left me unsettled.

Why would a beast from the shadow realm, known for killing wolves, not have murdered us all?

I carefully flipped through the pages of another book, this one much older and more delicate than the last. And that was where I found it—a page so timeworn I was worried it would crumble if I wasn't careful.

The text on the page was barely legible—most of it so faded there was nothing more than spots of distressed ink. But as I squinted, I could make out more words, though much of it was rune-line symbols I didn't understand.

But beneath that, the script spoke of lupus interfectorem's being called by dark magic—that much I already knew—but it was the words on the next line which made my blood run cold.

The page spoke of *two* kinds of lupus interfectorem, both living in the shadow realm. One was designed to protect the realm and prevent captured souls from escaping. These souls gave power to the darkness and served the lupus interfectorem with their ancient light. The light of wolves.

My fingers drummed on my chin. *Did that mean those who'd been taken throughout the ages were still in the realm, being held captive?*

I continued reading, despite feeling a sharp tug in the pit of my stomach.

The other kind of lupus interfectorem were hunters, called from the realm by dark forces who summoned their help in exchange for a soul. These monsters could travel realms when invited and would stop at nothing to destroy the one they were called to claim.

But they could only claim the soul of a wolf.

I sat down at the nearby table as fear raced up my spine. My head spun with so many disjointed thoughts as I tried to put the pieces of the puzzle together.

The lupus interfectorem hadn't killed Ember, not because it hadn't had a chance to before we'd shown up and destroyed it.

It hadn't killed her because it *couldn't.*

Not until her wolf had awakened.

I lowered my head, my shoulders sagging from the weight of what I'd just discovered. The night of the Fallen Moon was fast approaching.

Did this mean once Ember's wolf had surfaced, the lupus interfectorem would come for her?

I didn't know what to do, but I had to protect her. Somehow, I had to figure out a way to make sure she was safe, even if it meant sacrificing everything.

I knew I couldn't tell Grayson and Alex about what I'd found. There was no doubt as hard it would be, they'd have no choice but to banish her. As much as I could feel their attraction to her, I knew neither would risk the clan's future.

Not for anyone.

I sighed deeply and tucked the book into my coat. I had to make sure no one else ever uncovered what I had—at least not until the night of the Fallen Moon was over, and the clan had seen Ember's wolf.

Then they'd have to rally around her, one of their own, and help protect her from whatever might be coming for her.

And if they didn't, then I'd call on others who would, even if it meant that I too would be banished from my clan forever.

CHAPTER TWENTY

EMBER

"Come in!" came the muffled shout when I knocked on Cody's door an hour later.

I walked into what could only be described as a lavish mansion, decorated with rich mahogany tables and shelves. The sweeping staircase—which no doubt led to Cody's bedroom—was even lined with the expensive wood.

The thought of possibly climbing those stairs with him later in the evening sent my pulse into overdrive.

"Your home is so beautiful," I said, eyeing the large space as Cody greeted me in the foyer with a warm, gentle smile.

"Thank you. I spent a lot of time designing it. Figured I'd do it once and do it right." He took my hand in his and led me to one of the floor to ceiling windows. "I designed this room with the view in mind."

He drew aside the heavy curtain, and I gasped at the sight of the sun setting over the ocean, blazing a deep mix of gold and pink in the evening sky.

"It's stunning," I replied dreamily.

He stepped behind me, the heat of his muscular body warming my skin. "Not as beautiful as the view inside," he murmured, his lips grazing my neck. "When I'm near you, you're all I can see."

I turned toward him. I knew I'd get caught up in the spell of his beguiling gaze, but there was no avoiding it. "That sounds like such a line."

"You wound me," he replied teasingly, placing a hand over his heart. "I just tell it like I see it." He reached out and trailed his fingertips over my cheek. "And for the record, I've never had the desire to say that to *any* other woman."

He backed away, taking his heat with him, and I was thankful for it. If he'd looked at me with such longing for another second, I would've melted into a puddle on his shiny, hardwood floor.

"Wine?"

"Yes, please."

I followed him through a series of rooms until we ended up in a kitchen fit for a king. It was equipped with all the usual appliances, but unlike typical kitchens, everything in the room seemed oversized, from the towering pillars bracketing the entryway, to the chandeliers hanging above an elegant table that could easily fit twenty, to the ceiling soaring at least fifteen feet above our heads.

I'd been impressed by Grayson and Alex's place, but Cody's made theirs look like an average house in any suburban neighborhood.

He filled our glasses with red wine and then handed me one. "Cheers."

I lifted my glass and clinked it against his.

"So," he said as he led me to a leather sectional sofa in one of the living rooms. "I contemplated cooking for you tonight, but Grayson was right, I'm not the greatest chef."

"You certainly have the kitchen of one," I replied with a grin.

He chuckled softly. "I designed it for my mom. She used to live with me after my dad died. And damn, could she cook."

I was mesmerized by the light in his expression when he spoke of his mother. So, this was what it was like to have family memories that brought joy to your eyes.

"I had Liza pack up a picnic basket full of stuff. Thought maybe we could go for a drive and find a place to sit on a blanket and enjoy the sunset." He looked at me as though trying to figure out if I'd be game for outdoor eating. "Or is that too cheesy?"

"I think it sounds perfect."

He smiled. "Then, put your glass down, and let's get going. We can finish the bottle when we get back."

We headed back to the kitchen and then out a side door into a large garage.

"We'll take the Benza," he told me as he made a beeline for a shiny, black sports car on the opposite side of the grand space.

He opened the trunk and carefully placed the basket, along with a blanket, into it before opening my door.

"Such a gentleman."

"So does that mean I'm forgiven for the cheesy pick-up line?" He smirked playfully.

"Totally forgiven."

Minutes later, we were pulling onto a gravel road with the music turned up. It was such a normal thing to do, yet it felt strange doing it in a world so far from ordinary. The more I thought about it, the more questions I had.

"What kind of music do you like?"

Cody looked at me briefly, then returned his attention to the road and shifted gears as we picked up speed. "Rock, mainly. You?"

"Same. And some pop."

"You know, our worlds aren't entirely different," he replied. "We have cars and music just like humans do. And coffee shops, concerts, events. All the same things really, just different labels."

"Well, there's that whole thing where people can turn into wolves," I replied. "But otherwise, yes, *exactly* the same."

He chuckled at my sarcasm. "Okay, so maybe look at it this way. Yes, we can turn into wolves. It's like a second skin, a superpower, if you will. But humans evolved, right? So, we're all animals, but some of us can still connect to our origins."

It was such a simple way to explain a rather complicated world, but it worked.

"So, where are we headed?"

He turned the music down a notch, "I want to show you where I used to go when I needed to get away. I haven't been there in quite some time."

"You don't go there anymore?"

"Not often," he replied. "As a beta, I don't have a lot of time. Grayson likes to keep us busy. Since he and Alex became Alphas, they're both focused on fulfilling their fathers' wishes, especially Grayson."

I pursed my lips. "And what does that mean?"

"Their fathers were over-achievers. They had a vision for the way the clan *could* be. Acquire more territory, network with other clans, things like that." He turned a corner a little too sharply and instinctively reached out, placing his hand on my shoulder. "Sorry about that. I know what it's like to be in the passenger seat when someone's driving a little too fast. I'll slow down."

I loved the feel of his touch on me, but he wrapped his fingers back around the steering wheel and continued with what he was saying.

"I honestly think it'll be a great change. We've been closed off to other clans for so long that it'll be nice to be able to spend some with others."

"Like the Silver Creek clan?"

He frowned. "No. It'll be a cold day in hell before Grayson would ever consider aligning with them. They have history."

"What kind of history?" I couldn't help but ask.

All the talk about Silver Creek had piqued my curiosity. Selena had said they were one of the wealthier clans, so wouldn't it make sense for the Thunder Cove clan to network with them?

He must have sensed my curiosity because he continued, "History that doesn't get easily erased. No matter how much time passes." He slowed down as another car appeared in front of us. "I understand where Grayson is coming from. It isn't my story to tell, so I won't speak on it. But I'd probably feel the same way if I was him. We're almost there."

He turned down a side road, and I watched as the sun faded off in the distance. Minutes later, we stopped and got out. I glanced around as he opened the trunk and pulled out the basket and blanket.

All around me were sandy trails, leading down to the beach. When Cody joined me, leaning in for a sweet kiss, I wanted nothing more than to let go of the heaviness perched on my chest like a bucket of bricks and enjoy the view.

But thinking about Cody only made it harder to forget what Selena and I had uncovered. The thought of possibly bringing danger to men who'd been so kind to me made my heart ache.

"Come on," Cody said as he grabbed my hand and tugged me along one of the pathways. Once we reached the shore, he set the blanket down on the soft sand, and I joined him.

"When I needed to get away from it all, I'd come down here and sit for hours. Nothing like the ocean to clear your mind." He reached into the picnic basket and removed the food as he spoke. Tender meat and breads, olives and peppers, exotic cheeses, and to top it off, a bottle of wine.

"It's a lovely spot," I replied. "So peaceful."

And it was. Only a few feet away, the ocean waves were icy blue and folding over on themselves as they rushed up to the shore. The cliffs, off in the distance, were stark black in comparison, and beyond, the sun was dipping into the horizon —painting the perfect scenery for a romantic picnic, just like this.

"So, tell me about you. I know you're one of the betas, and it's obvious you mean a lot to Grayson and Alex, but what about before all that. It must have been incredible growing up in a place like this. With so many realms and places to explore."

I didn't mention the shadow realm or that I'd gone to see an elder who claimed I'd been marked. I'd promised Selena I wouldn't say a word, and after all she'd done for me, I had to keep my word.

Still, I was curious about what realms Cody had explored. The fact that so many different magical creatures lived within their own territories was more than a little intriguing.

He smiled. "My mom was what you'd call one of those over-protective parents. She'd never let me stray too far until I got much older. When we were kids, and Grayson and Alex would go off on some wild adventure into another realm, I'd have to come up with some rather creative ways to get away with them."

"Like what?"

He nudged my leg. "The usual. Sneak out through the bedroom window after I'd stuffed my bed with enough sheets to look like I was sleeping." He chuckled. "Then, she got wise to that, so I had to bribe my sister to cover for me."

His expression darkened just a little when he mentioned Trinity. I longed to ask him more about her, but I hesitated before veering into another direction.

"Have you been to many realms, then?"

"No," he replied. "That's playing with fire."

"Well you can't just leave it at that," I countered with a smile, popping a piece of cheese in my mouth. "Do tell."

"Most of the realms are too dangerous to enter. Or too unknown. So, we mainly stick to shifter realms. Thankfully, the portals are marked with the insignia of whatever supernatural lives there, so at least we aren't wandering into places without knowing what to expect."

That answered one of the many burning questions I had. Ever since Grayson had mentioned how vampires dominated multiple realms, I'd wondered how they knew whether something deadly existed beyond one of the portals.

"Even with the markings, sometimes it's hard to know whether we'd be welcome or not. Take the Fae, for example." He chortled softly. "Their realm was enchanting. I've never seen so much beauty in one place in my life. But Grayson and I weren't there longer than twenty minutes before some sort of colorful creature tried to kill us."

"Oh, wow." I reached for another piece of cheese. "So, how many shifter realms have you found so far?"

A long pause followed, and my question hung there, heavy and awkward.

"A few. The last one we explored was a were-bear realm. They were very welcoming, but their customs are rather outdated."

"How so?"

"They follow a rather strict hierarchy." He opened the wine, poured some into a plastic glass, and then handed it to me before filling his own. "The women live to serve their mates. They seemed happy doing it, but it was all a little too old-fashioned for me."

I couldn't help the smile on my face at his words. And I was thankful to hear them. Since their clan was led by two Alphas, I'd wondered if women had a voice or if they were merely silent members of a clan where men made the rules, and the women just followed them. I recalled how Selena had said something about how Alphas made rules without having to explain the reasons behind them.

"I met Selena today," I told him, and he cocked an eyebrow.

"And how did that go? My cousin can be a lot of energy, but she always means well. She's got a big heart."

I peered at him "She was really nice. And I can tell she cares about you a great deal."

He nodded. "She's a great girl. We grew up together. She and my sister are close. I wish Trinity would come home."

Now seemed like the best time to finally ask more about her.

"Do you have any ideas where your sister might be?"

He averted his eyes, staring off at the dwindling sunset as a gust of wind blew across the sand, ruffling his short, golden-brown hair. "I'm not sure. Trinity isn't someone who'd venture off without reason." He shrugged. "I'm sure I'll see her again one day."

I got the feeling he knew more about Trinity's whereabouts than he was letting on, but I didn't press.

"And the other realms? What did you find in those besides were-bears?" I asked, changing the subject when I saw that faraway look in his eyes.

"One was Silver Creek's realm. My dad brought me there to meet the Alpha's son. It was a place right out of a storybook. I loved going there as a kid."

I thought again about Selena's mention of the Silver Creek clan's wealth, but before I could ask more, he continued.

"And another realm belonged to dragons."

"*Dragons*? Were they friendly?"

"Very. They're always welcoming to other shifters." He cleared his throat as if he had something more to say but wasn't sure if he should. "We stay away from most other shifter realms. Our clan has been to war with many of them when our fathers were alive, and even though it was a long time ago and a new generation leads them, we keep our distance."

The sun was now well below the horizon, and when I tilted my head back, I saw the stars glittering against the velveteen darkness.

"What about you?" Cody asked, his face bathed in starlight. He reached over to brush a strand of my hair away from my face. "You told us you were left when you were a baby. I can't imagine how hard it was for you... growing up without parents. How did you survive?"

I glanced at him out of the corner of my eye and saw the solemn look on his face.

"No, it wasn't easy," I answered honestly. I closed my eyes momentarily before opening them again.

His question had hit me like a sucker-punch, low and deep.

"But I survived as anyone else would. I kept thinking life would get better once I was on my own. That when I was an adult, I could make my own way. And I did."

My words brought a smile to his lips, the moon's gleam highlighting his jaw. "You certainly did. And I'm so glad it led you here."

"Well," I responded. "Technically, *you* brought me here against my will."

I leaned toward him, my arms snaking around his neck. "But I'm happy you did."

I drew in a sharp breath, and a jet of fire licked down my spine when he responded to my touch by pulling me down on top of him.

His hands wandered across my body as though he had every right to do it—as if I was his woman. They finally rested on my ass, and when he squeezed, holding me tightly against him, I felt the swell of his erection.

"I'll always be there for you," he murmured against my cheek, his hands still cupping my ass as I pressed against him. "No matter what."

I lifted my face to him, and another rush of heat raced between my thighs at the intensity in his gaze. I wanted to weep at his words. I'd never had anyone look at me that way before or make such promises, and I wondered if he'd still be whispering those words against my skin if he knew how much trouble I could bring to his clan.

Under the moonlight, he looked positively stunning, from the sexy grin, which played on his lips to the slight tension along his perfectly cut jaw. He reached out, and his thumb wandered upward, caressing my lower lip.

"And don't ever forget it."

Then his arms banded around me possessively as he flipped me over on my back, and I let out a squeal at the suddenness of his movements.

"Ever."

He kissed my temple, my jaw. Then his lips were on my neck as my fingers made their way into his hair. He swept his lips over my chin and up to my mouth. Then there was no more need for words.

The kiss was all-consuming, and my head swam with the heady sensation of being tucked safely beneath such a strong, glorious man. He moaned against me when my fingernails slowly trailed down his shoulders. The kiss deepened, his tongue snaking against mine wildly, his teeth grazing over my jaw and throat before returning to my mouth.

It was a kiss filled with urgency, with an unstoppable need to satisfy the deep ache burning in our bellies and lighting our hearts on fire.

I wanted him more than I'd ever wanted anyone. When he lifted, kneeling above me as he tugged off his t-shirt, I was ready to beg just to feel his cock inside of me.

"I want you, Cody. I want you so badly."

I lifted my shirt, and he helped me pull it off, dropping it on the blanket as I wiggled out of my jeans. His eyes glinted in the moonlight, and even in the growing darkness, I knew they were filled with hunger—the same I felt for him.

He gently ran his fingertips along the edge of my bra, making my breath freeze in my lungs. His head dipped to press hot kisses to my covered breasts. A moan escaped me. Eager to feel his mouth on me, I reached behind me and unfastened my bra. Then he was there, right where I needed him, nipping at my newly uncovered flesh.

Heat rushed south, making me whimper. Cody's hands trailed down my sides slowly until his fingers dipped into the waistband of my panties. Gradually, he slipped the fabric down my legs until they were low enough for me to kick them off.

Shifting away from me, his hungry gaze raked over my skin.

He unzipped his jeans as I lay naked between his legs, and I was thankful for the bravery the darkness gave me as I watched him finish stripping.

Then he was whispering against my cheek something about how he wanted to take his time with me, to go slow. I quivered as his hands squeezed my breasts before they slid lower, lifting me just a little until he was squeezing my ass.

"You're so beautiful," he murmured against my lips when I reached down and wrapped my hand around his cock. He used his firm grip to grind his body against mine, his hands on my ass, sliding higher until he was cradling my shoulders, his cock hard and ready.

"So perfect."

He kissed me deeper, merciless, claiming my lips and tongue so completely that for a moment, I could barely breathe, as a tremor of desire raced over my chest, between my breasts, and down to my thighs.

Within minutes, I felt the tip of his cock press against my pussy, and I spread my legs wider, spread-eagle. I was so wet when the head pushed between my lips, there was no struggle.

"God, I want you," he whispered against my mouth. "Every day. Just like this."

I cried out when his cock slid inside of me, my pussy now wrapped tightly around his smooth shaft. His thrusts came hard and fast, and it awakened my body in ways I'd never known.

Somewhere between impatiently working his hands all over me as I clenched around his cock, and the whisper of his kiss against my neck, he'd forgotten all about going slow.

But I didn't mind at all.

I arched my back as his lips claimed my breasts, his mouth moving from one nipple to the other. His teeth grazed my sensitive skin, and I whimpered with desire when his lips dragged between them, leaving a trail of fire in their wake.

"Oh, Cody," I said breathlessly. "Oh my God."

He lowered his mouth to my ear, his words nothing more than a rumble against my skin. "I'm never going to get enough of you."

"Don't... don't stop," I groaned, my voice frantic. "Please."

And he didn't, not until he took us both to the edge. I cried out first, arching up beneath him, my hands clutching the blanket, the material caught between my fingers as his lips returned to mine, his kiss as hard and brutal as his thrusts.

Then I cried out again as another streak of fire raced through my body and tension filled my limbs. My pussy hummed over the fullness of his cock buried deep inside of me, and I matched his pace.

My head was spinning, and I knew I was moments away from losing control as my hips moved back and forth, arching up to meet his, moving faster and harder with every motion.

I was at his mercy, begging him for release. My body responded to his every touch, whether from his lips, his fingers, his cock. Then he abandoned my breasts and gasped against my shoulder, his breath hot and harsh on my skin.

"Ember..."

There was a new urgency to his strokes, a warning he couldn't hold off much longer. My body shuddered when the first wave of another orgasm thundered through my body.

Then his lips were back on mine, muffling my cries. When

he released me and his gaze locked on mine, I knew there was no turning back for him either.

He lifted himself to his knees, gripping my hips and pulling them toward him until I wrapped my legs around his back.

Then he took me where I longed to go, the pressure building inside of me until I was overwhelmed with pleasure—every touch, every thrust, invading my senses as everything else faded into the background.

"Come for me again, Ember."

He didn't need to ask twice as I rode the wave of pleasure, his cock seeming to get harder and thicker as he bucked wildly against me. His hands moved from my hips to my ass, and when he jerked me forward, my muscles contracted. I threw my head back as I cried out, the fire that raged inside me demanding release.

He held himself above me, watching my face as I came, refusing to let up. In the next heartbeat, after he'd made sure I was fully satisfied, he pulled out as a possessive growl ripped from his throat, drowning out my whimpers, my body still trembling with the aftershocks of my orgasm.

"Baby... you okay?" Cody lay alongside me. He reached for me as if he needed to know I had no regrets.

I turned onto my side to face him and kissed him gently, sweetly as I caught my breath, my body limp with satisfaction.

"That was amazing, Cody."

Then, suddenly, there was a sense of him letting go of something as he drew me into his arms, so my head rested on his chest, his fingers tracing lines over my shoulder.

"I meant what I said," he whispered into my hair. "I'll always be here for you. So please, just let me."

I tucked a chunk of hair behind my ear and nodded wordlessly as my body relaxed fully for the first time since I'd awoken in this world.

And under the twinkling stars with the ocean's melody

playing in the background, all thoughts of the dangers that lay ahead faded from my mind.

In the few moments, before we made our way back up the sandy bank to his car and he drove me home, I was just a girl cradled in the arms of a boy she was falling in love with.

CHAPTER TWENTY-ONE

EMBER

It was the night of the Fallen Moon, and I woke up sweaty, my body filled with fear about what was to come. Now that the day was finally here, the reality was setting in. Outside, the sky was clear, with only a few clouds bunching near the horizon.

I threw off the covers and quickly got dressed. I needed to release all the nervous energy crawling over my skin.

A few minutes later, I found myself pounding the pavement. I ran as fast and as hard as I could until my chest felt as though it might explode if I didn't slow down.

My mind drifted back to the night before when Cody had made love to me on the shore. I replayed the scene. His passionate kisses, his possessive touch, his promise that he would always be there for me. Then he'd asked me to come home with him, but I hadn't. I needed distance to clear my head and prepare myself for what the Fallen Moon might bring, so I told him I was tired, and he didn't question me.

Instead, he'd dropped me off and pressed a heated goodnight kiss to my lips, which told me I wouldn't have gotten much sleep had I gone home with him.

I came to a halt, lowered my hands to my knees, and sucked in several breaths as I tried to calm my pounding heart. Whatever I'd hoped running a couple of blocks would do to release my tension, it hadn't.

Thoughts of the creature from the shadow realm sent a shiver down my back. I wanted my wolf to awaken, but knowing the beast might be able to destroy me once she surfaced made my blood run cold.

Selena had reassured me a shadow creature likely couldn't enter another magical realm. If she was right, as long as I didn't return to the human world, maybe I'd be safe.

Still, I couldn't shake the harrowing tone in Elgin's voice when he'd told us the wolf slayer wouldn't stop until it had claimed my soul.

"Ember? You okay?"

I turned toward the sound of Grayson's voice. As he came closer, the sun brought out the flecks of silver in his hair. I hadn't noticed them before.

"Yeah, I'm fine," I panted. "I thought I'd go for a run, but this is as far as I got before my legs gave out. I hope my wolf isn't this out of shape."

"Weakness is a human trait," he replied, eyeing me as though I was dressed in some sexy get-up rather than a pair of shorts and a T-shirt with sweat dripping down my forehead. "Your wolf will be a lot stronger."

"Yeah, yeah, I get it. You don't like humans. You need to get some new material."

He cocked an eyebrow but then decided to change the subject. "You eat yet? I'm headed down to the docks for the morning fish fry if you want to join me."

I scrunched my nose. "Isn't it a little too early for fish?"

"And yet another human trait," he replied. The intentionally, overly serious expression on his face made me chuckle. "Once you shift, you'll want meat all day, every day." He tugged me along. "You can thank me later."

We ambled toward where I assumed the docks were. It was in a different part of town than I'd been to before, but as we crested the hill, I gasped.

A long, green patch of grass stretched outward until it reached rows of trees that bloomed with summer vitality. From there, the town unfolded with roads winding further down until they reached the water.

"Pretty, isn't it?"

Pretty didn't begin to describe how gorgeous this side of town was. It was a view more breathtaking than any postcard. It reminded me of the night before when Cody and I had stood overlooking the sandbanks.

The ocean was as blue as a sapphire, its waves crashing against red cliffs that went on for miles.

"You'll love the boardwalk," Grayson murmured with pride as he led me down a sandy path. "Farmers' markets are set up here every summer. You'll find heirloom apples, pickled herrings, and even mayflower honey. My stomach is growling just at the thought of it."

Scratch off pickled herrings, and it did sound good.

"And this week, some of our best artists are giving classes. In case, you'd like to learn to paint."

I thought about the day I'd seen easels scattered around a room in his house when I'd first awoken and tried to escape. The possibility it was Grayson who'd created them hadn't even crossed my mind. For some reason, he hardly seemed the type.

"Do you paint?"

His eyes dropped to the ground beneath our feet, and I saw how he clenched his jaw as if my question had embarrassed him. I nudged him with my elbow.

"Hello? Anybody home?"

He smirked and rolled his eyes. "Yeah, I paint. If you can call it that."

"I saw some of your paintings," I replied. "They were beautiful."

His expression softened a bit, but he eyed me suspiciously, as though he wasn't sure whether I was pulling his leg or not.

"My mom is an artist. A very gifted one. People come from all over the realm for the chance to have her create their portraits. I'll never be that talented or anything, but it's a good...outlet."

I smiled. "I bet. Maybe I'll give it a try sometime. I could certainly use an outlet."

He eyed me again, but this time it seemed different, as though he recognized something in my expression he hadn't seen before.

"I could teach you."

The offer took me by surprise. "Really? You'd do that?"

"Sure," he replied with a shrug. "Why not? It's not like I can turn you into a Leonardo da Cinco or anything, but it could be fun."

I cocked an eyebrow. "You mean Leonardo da Vinci."

He tilted his head, his face wreathed in confusion. "Who?"

"Never mind," I replied, laughing. Some similarities between our worlds were just a little too strange to even try to understand.

I took a deep breath as we soaked in the beauty around us.

"Your home is such a captivating place."

I peered out at the water, sparkling like diamonds, and my eyes welled up with tears I didn't understand. I did my best to hide them from Grayson, but he reached out and ran his hand down my back.

"Has anyone ever told you you're a bit of a crybaby?"

I snorted through my tears, and he wrapped his arm around my shoulder as we looked at the softly, rolling waves.

"You should've grown up in a place like this. But you're here now, and that's all that matters."

I let myself stay nestled in the crook of his arm for a moment longer, breathing in his masculine scent. Grayson was a confusing man. One moment, he looked at me as though he wasn't sure what to make of me, but the next, he was a gentle giant.

"Let's go eat. We need you at your strongest tonight."

He released me, and we made our way to the fish fry. It was a giant setup with dozens of tables and a large, round platform in the middle filled with fryers. I had to admit, it smelled amazing.

"Alpha! It's so good to have you join us!" The greeting came from a beautiful woman with an hourglass figure, which would make any woman envious. The shape of her face was equally as pretty with a slender nose, full lips, and the kind of complexion that didn't need makeup.

"Hi Laura," Grayson replied as she sashayed up to him.

I couldn't help but notice the way her hips swayed with extra *oomph*, her tiny waist highlighted by a white belt and her navy-blue dress.

"How've you been?"

She eyed him like she was starving, and he was a juicy piece of meat. It made my stomach churn in a way I wasn't happy about.

"I've been great," she murmured, her gaze locked on his face and her eyelashes fluttering like two butterflies who were finally emerging from their cocoon. "Just missing you. It's been a while. What are you doing later?"

I bristled at the comment—actually, at the entire situation and the weird tension happening between them. And despite knowing how dumb it would make me look, I stepped forward and extended my hand.

"Hi Laura, I'm Ember. It's nice to meet you. Since Grayson didn't introduce us, I thought I would."

I eyed Grayson and saw he was smirking in a way that let me know he knew I was more than a little annoyed.

Laura didn't return my gesture. Instead, her lips curled up as though she was being poisoned by the sight of me. Then her eyes darted to Grayson as if to say, *'why is she with you?'* before she took a few steps back.

"Who's this?"

Grayson chuckled softly but left me to fend for myself.

"I'm sure you've heard the rumor about a halfling being brought here." It was a statement, not a question. "Unfortunately, the rumor is true. And you're looking at her."

That elicited a reaction I could only describe as horrified, and Laura made no effort to hide it. Her frantic gaze flew to Grayson, her expression filled with anger.

"I didn't want to believe it," she growled, the flirty softness in her voice replaced with a hard edge. "You... *you* feel the same way I do about humans. Why would you ever bring one here?"

I didn't wait for Grayson to reply. I wasn't even sure he would've, considering he seemed to be enjoying the interaction a little too much.

"Oh, you misheard," I replied all matter-of-factly, though I knew full well she'd intended to be hurtful. "I'm a *halfling*, not a human. I know, it can get rather confusing. I'm still getting used to it myself." I took a step toward Grayson and wrapped my arm around his bicep. "Your Alpha tells me once my wolf surfaces, I'm going to want to eat meat all day long." I smiled as though I'd been suddenly struck with the most incredible thought. "So, I guess that means you'll be seeing me here at the fish fry all the time! Maybe we can sit together sometime."

I allowed myself the satisfaction of enjoying her scowl, and then I looked up at Grayson.

"Thanks for inviting me to join you for breakfast. That fish smells amazing. Ready to eat?"

He gazed down at me, his smile getting bigger, and nodded.

"Have a great day, Laura." Then he slid his hand into mine and led me to a table in the middle of the crowded room.

I felt the weight of eyes on me and the energy change as we sat down, but Grayson didn't seem to notice.

Or maybe he didn't care.

"I knew you could handle yourself," he murmured, scanning my face. "You didn't need me to intervene. Laura is all bark and no bite, anyway."

"Who was she?" I asked. "I mean, who was she *to you?*"

"We dated for a few months a year or so ago. It was nothing. She wanted more than I could give her, so we ended things."

I nodded, not at all surprised. "The way she looks at you... I don't think she's over you yet."

"Laura was in love with the idea of power. She knew I'd be Alpha one day. We weren't meant for one another. I wanted one thing while she wanted another."

"And what was it that *you* wanted? You said before you didn't believe in fated mates, so obviously, it wasn't that."

"I don't really know," he replied, and I could tell it was an honest response. "I've never liked the idea there was only one person meant for each of us. That always seemed so... bleak. Depressing."

"I agree," I replied. "But I'm not exactly experienced in the love and relationship department. I've dated a few guys, but nothing ever seemed to work out. Oh, my God." I turned at the delicious smell suddenly invading my senses and saw a man headed our way with two heaping plates of cooked fish.

Grayson laughed. "I told you. Maybe it won't even take the Fallen Moon to convince your wolf to wake up. Maybe all she needs is a good feast of Thunder Bay fish."

I pursed my lips at his statement and eyed the platters of fish being set down in front of us.

"Anything else, Alpha?" the man asked.

"Just a couple glasses of water and maybe some extra napkins for this one."

The man chuckled. "I'll be right back."

"Dig in." Grayson's beautiful, amber eyes bore into mine in a dare. "You'll need your energy."

I filled my fork with the white meat, and when I tasted it, I nearly moaned. It was wonderfully flavored and so tender and flaky. Within minutes, I'd devoured every piece while he was still working on finishing his.

"I swear, my appetite has changed so much since I got here. I'm going to end up gaining so much weight if I stay."

"If you stay?" He seemed to ponder my words for a moment. "You won't be happy if you go back, not after your wolf surfaces. You'd never be able to shift again. Not in that world."

I looked at him, puzzled. "But you shifted the night you saved me."

"We had no choice. We're much stronger as wolves. But no, we *don't* shift in the human world. Not that I go there unless I have to. Most humans don't know about us, and if they did, it could pose a problem we don't need."

"You said before humans are weak. You made that very clear. So, what would you have to be worried about? I mean, other than them possibly shooting you."

"It isn't their guns we're worried about, Ember."

"Then what is —"

"Humans would never leave us alone if they knew about us. Our younger wolves would enter the human world to explore, only to find themselves taken against their will. Turned into nothing more than experiments."

I knew what he was saying was true. If humans discovered the existence of supernaturals, I had no doubt they'd do exactly that.

Then I thought about the shadow creature and what it could do to the human population should it choose to show itself.

"The thing that attacked me... that wolf slayer... it can't attack humans?"

"Just wolves," he replied, confirming what I'd read. "Humans have nothing to worry about." He glanced down at my empty plate. "Do you want a second helping before we go?"

"No thanks," I replied, sitting back and rubbing my stomach. "I'm so full. I couldn't take another bite."

That made him smile, and some of the shadows lifted from his eyes. "You excited for tonight? I can't imagine shifting for the first time at twenty-five. It's like losing your virginity."

"Not twenty-five for a few more weeks," I replied playfully. "And yes, I'm excited. But I'm also extremely nervous. Thanks for reminding me. And not sure if you realize this, but to girls, losing our virginities is never fun."

He laughed. But then he reached across the table and took my hands in his momentarily, his expression turning serious. "You're going to be just fine. No one has ever died from shifting. It actually feels amazing."

I gave him a half-ass grin which made him squeeze a little tighter before he let go.

"You ready to go?"

I nodded and stood up as the man from earlier returned to clear the table.

As Grayson and I strolled along the sandy boardwalk on the way back to the main street, Grayson promised once my wolf awakened, I'd never be the same. I knew that come what may under the light of the Fallen Moon, my life had already been changed forever.

CHAPTER TWENTY-TWO

EMBER

L ater that evening, I tried not to stare as Grayson undressed, but I couldn't help myself. His ass was tight muscle, just like the rest of him, and the cock that bounced out of his jeans was more than impressive.

It wasn't the first time I'd seen him naked, but now certainly felt different than the night in the woods when he and the others had rescued me.

It was only a short time ago, yet it felt like years. Now, it felt like I'd known him all my life.

Alongside him, Cody tugged off his shirt, as did Alex. My mind raced at the thought of undressing in front of the three of them—only Cody had seen me naked— but when I unzipped my jeans, they turned away. I smiled at the gesture and silently thanked them for making it easier on me.

A few minutes later, Cody had spread out a blanket for the two of us, much like he had the night before, while Alex and Grayson remained standing. I trembled nervously and made myself as small as possible, my arms crossed over my chest.

Cody scooted closer to me and drew me into the shelter of his side.

"It won't be long now," Grayson said as he peered up at the dark sky in anticipation. "The clan is on their way. Ember, when you feel the change come, just let it happen. Don't fight it."

"You have nothing to worry about," Alex added. "Remember what we told you. The shift feels amazing. It doesn't hurt. And Cody will be right by your side tonight, Ember."

They'd told me the plan, so I was as prepared as I could be. I knew Alex and Grayson would be close by, but they also had others to worry about—shifters who hadn't experienced a fallen moon before, as well as a handful of elders who were weak and anxious to be healed.

But suddenly, the thought of all the adult members of their clan making their way toward us made me tremble.

I wasn't sure if my wolf even existed, much less if she'd dare to surface.

What if she didn't?

The full attention of the clan would be on me—the weird, half-human, half-wolf girl who their Alphas and beta had brought into their realm. I knew they wouldn't accept me if I didn't shift, so what would that mean for my friendship with Cody? With Alex? With Grayson?

Within minutes, the space was filled with naked shifters as they waited for the Fallen Moon to appear. The air was bursting with excitement, and even though my stomach prickled with nerves, I felt a smile grace my lips as I peered around.

The clan cared deeply for one another. It was evident in the way they held hands, hugged, or helped one another get ready for the shift. I saw what I assumed to be mates embracing, and friends already celebrating what was to come. And there was Selena, off in the distance, looking as beautiful as she did the other day now standing with a group of women. I considered waving to get her attention, but something gave me pause. I was nervous—*so* nervous—so maybe the fewer people surrounding me, the better.

As I sat on the ground with my arms crossed over me, I took a deep breath to steady my shaky hands.

"Thunder Cove clan," Grayson began as he made his way to the front of the gathering. "This is the night we've been waiting for."

There was no denying it—Grayson was a vision to behold as he stood, naked, in front of hundreds of people who hung on his every word.

He embodied power and authority from head to toe—from his broad shoulders to his legs thick and corded with strength.

"Tonight, we'll be blessed with the power of our ancestors. Under the Fallen Moon, we'll be at our full strength, so embrace it!"

The crowd cheered, and Grayson's grin grew slowly into a broad smile.

They loved him, that was obvious. As Alex joined him, the two embraced momentarily before Alex said a few words about the future of their clan and how proud he was of them. For once, I felt part of something larger than life.

I rose to my feet, standing with the others, and when I glanced over at Cody, who was now a few feet away, I saw he was beaming as he applauded his Alphas. The crowd was in an absolute frenzy.

Suddenly, I sensed someone behind me. When I spun around, I came face to face with Rylen.

He leaned in close to me, so close I could feel his breath on my face. "Good luck tonight. You'll need it."

Something inside of me tightened at the cruel edge in his voice, and when I raised my eyes to his, I saw how his glinted with danger.

I should've flinched away, but instead, I remained rooted in place. I wasn't sure why my mere presence seemed to anger him so much, but I wasn't going to let him get the best of me. Not on such an important night.

"Thank you," I replied coolly, never breaking eye contact. "I appreciate it."

He stared me down a moment longer as an uneasy feeling rippled through my body. Then to my relief, he finally took a step back, disappearing into the crowd.

My breathing grew frantic now that I was alone. Panic flooded my veins.

Cody made his way back to me. "Hey, sorry. I won't leave your side again."

"It's okay," I said in a shaky voice as I tilted my head back to peer at the sky.

One by one, stars filled the sky like silver, sparkling jewels on a queen's crown, growing impossibly brighter as they over-powered the shadows and lit up the night. I was mesmerized by the glorious tapestry of colors being woven above as the moon began to expand. Within seconds, it felt as if the energy surrounding us began to waver, suddenly alive with raw electricity.

I reached out, frantically searching for Cody, and he pulled my trembling body into his arms. "I've got you," he whispered into my hair. "I won't let you out of my sight. Just breathe."

Then I felt it.

It started as a soft vibration, washing over my skin like a cool autumn breeze that kissed my cheek and grew stronger with every second. My skin pebbled, and my nipples hardened as the sensation increased, spreading out until my entire body quivered.

I let out a groan, not because I felt pain but rather because of the thrill that came with the burst of power flowing through my veins. It was intoxicating, a rush of fire lighting up my body with an intensity that caused me to fall to my knees. My muscles grew tense as heat pulsed down my neck, across my stomach, and then pooled between my thighs.

"Breathe. Just breathe. And let go." Cody was on his knees alongside me, just as he'd promised.

I watched his body begin to change, and when my own transformation became even more intense, I closed my eyes and let go.

They were right; it felt amazing. As my body began to change, any fear I'd been holding onto vanished along with any semblance of my human form.

My muscles grew and strengthened as my wolf's power rippled down my spine and stomach. Her energy quickly gave form to a bushy tail and underbelly. Within minutes, I'd transformed from a human into a she-wolf.

The moment the change was complete, I peered up into the bright night sky and howled.

It was a sound that had been a mere whisper burning inside of me for as long as I could remember. I suddenly understood why my heart had been beating to the rhythm of a broken melody for so long.

My wolf had been forced to stay silent, to hide. But as my memory sharpened, I realized it hadn't always been that way. She'd tried to rise to the surface many times when I was younger, but I'd forced her to submit to my human side.

To quiet her call to me, to conceal herself in a world I knew would never accept us.

Memories of being no older than ten or eleven came rushing back—a small child who felt the power of a wolf streaking through her veins but didn't know what it meant or what to do about it.

My foster parents had heartlessly believed my behavior was nothing more than the tantrums of an undisciplined child and so punished me every time my power began to surface.

Eventually, my wolf had been trained to stay quiet, buried so deep down she became nothing more than a shadow that could never fully form.

And then I'd forgotten all about her when I turned into a teen and then a woman.

But under the light of a fallen moon, in a world of magic, she could show herself in all her glory.

And she did.

As we stood in the center of a growing crowd, she refused to hold back. I was sure her howl reached the heavens.

When she was done, she let me know she was in no way satisfied but it would do for now.

Through her eyes, I scanned the area, mesmerized by everything I saw. The colors of the night were so vivid, so clear—shades of greens, blues, and purples, as vibrant as a glorious painting. When I turned my head, I met the curious eyes of many wolves as the moon shone her silvery light over the crowd.

Every one of my senses was in overdrive. The sharp, sweet scent of the pine trees off in the distance filled my nostrils, as did the rich aroma of the cool earth beneath my feet. It reminded me of the rainy days of my youth when I'd spent hours outside under clearing skies all alone, hoping for a rainbow.

But I wasn't alone anymore.

I took a tentative step forward, adjusting to the weight of this new form. My balance was slightly off but only for a few seconds. I settled into it quickly, as though I'd shifted a thousand times before.

"Ember, can you hear me?"

Cody had explained how shifters communicated, but nothing could've prepared me for the way his deep voice ignited a fire inside of me when I heard him in my head. I turned to him, my wolf facing his for the first time, I felt as though he was all I could see. His silvery fur was stunning, and I longed to nuzzle against him.

"*Yes,*" I replied, my mind opening to allow my thoughts to spread out like fireflies floating on a breeze.

I could sense when others read my mind, and for a moment, it felt far too invasive. In turn, I was able to hear their thoughts, though there were so many of them surrounding me it was impossible to make out what they were thinking.

I closed the connection, surprised by the ease with which I controlled it. All it took was a bit of concentration, and I could open and close it as quickly as a human opened and closed a door.

Cody nudged me with his muzzle. "*Let me hear you.*"

I wanted to tell him my thoughts were running too rampant and wild to share with anyone. I needed time to process what was happening, but he nudged me again, this time more firmly. "*You can choose just to let me in and no one else. Focus on me.*"

I did as he told me to, and for a moment, the sound of a hundred murmurs crowded my brain. I closed my eyes and focused my thoughts on his energy. When I opened my eyes, his voice was the only one I could hear.

"*That's my girl. How are you feeling?*"

A single word surfaced as I reached a paw out and stroked his silky coat.

"*Alive.*"

It was the word that continued to burn through my mind as we took off, racing toward the forest trail.

I kept up easily, Cody's pace only slowing when we reached what looked like a lake. I scanned the scenery, breathing in the scent of damp moss, wet tree trunks, and flowers. The forest was alive with life.

"*Look,*" he told me. "*Look how beautiful your wolf is.*"

I followed his gaze aimed at the water, and my reflection glinted in the soft current.

I couldn't look away from the creature who stared back at

me. Illuminated by the silver-cream of the Fallen Moon, she was striking with her bluish-gray coat that shimmered in the light.

But I saw much more than the beauty of her fur.

Her eyes sparkled with the glow of freedom, of a wild heart finally allowed to follow the call of the wind.

It was more than a reflection that stared back at me.

I was staring into my very soul.

I whined, a mixture of overwhelming joy at meeting her and sadness that she'd been caged for so long.

"Come with me," Cody murmured, refusing to let me get swept away in regret over lost time.

I faithfully followed. As we covered the distance, I picked up the scent of something savory and far more mouth-watering than any flavor I'd ever known.

We raced toward it, and within minutes I saw it. A white-tailed deer stalked the forest a few feet away.

I could smell the tender meat and the soft bone marrow as we moved closer and waited for the perfect moment to strike. That moment came sooner than expected. The deer turned in our direction, its eyes sweeping the trees before settling on me, recognition registering in its glinting orbs.

It knew its life would be over in seconds and didn't bother putting up a chase.

The human side of me suddenly tried to reason with my wolf, to remind her we liked our meat medium-well done and certainly didn't want to be the one to butcher it. Still, the voice was drowned out by the heady scent of my prey, and I lunged forward, tackling the deer to the ground and sinking my teeth into its throat.

Thankfully, there was one thing my wolf and I agreed on; we didn't want to make it suffer. So I was relieved to feel it quickly go limp beneath my weight.

I was ravenous. Hungrier than I'd ever been before, but it didn't take long before the meat was gone, and I was sated.

I glanced back, suddenly embarrassed I hadn't shared the feast with Cody, but I saw in his eyes that he was more than a little proud of what I'd just done on my own.

"Are you tired, or do you want to run some more?" he asked me.

"I feel like I could run all night," I replied.

He chuckled, a deeper tone than when in his human form.

"In that case, try to keep up."

He took off, and I sprinted after him, my legs moving at a speed I wouldn't have thought possible. And even though I was anything but light, I felt weightless, graceful.

We ran for hours as he showed me around the clan territory, wandering where no human would ever go. We raced through dense brush, crossed narrow wooden bridges, and scampered over moss softened rocks and stones smoothed with age. Then we dashed back under the canopy of the largest trees I'd ever seen.

Finally, we came to a halt, both of us breathless and over-whelmed with the power coursing through our bodies.

"I've never felt so complete. So truly happy."

I felt the heat of his wolf as he nuzzled against me.

"I knew it. From the day I saw you, I knew you were meant to be here. With me. With this clan."

Suddenly, I thought about Alex and Grayson and how we'd left them behind. I longed to see them in their true forms and to run alongside them. And to let them see me. To see who I truly was.

Cody placed a paw on my back, and I realized I hadn't closed the connection. *"Don't worry. You'll see them soon. A lot was going on for them tonight as well. Let's go."*

Embarrassment coursed through me that he knew what I'd been thinking, but when he stroked my back again, I knew he understood how much they *all* meant to me.

As he led me back toward the central part of town, I couldn't stop thinking about how I wanted the night to end.

Not with me lying in bed alone, reflecting on the wonder of the evening.

But with me wrapped in the arms of three men who made my heart flutter.

"Are you sure that's what you want?" Cody's voice reached out to me once again.

His tone sounded off when his words materialized in my mind. But I wasn't sure why.

"I'm so sorry. I keep forgetting about how the connection works. My thoughts wander and—"

I stopped moving when he did, in a private little alcove. No one was around. and within minutes he'd transformed back to his human self.

"Wipe everything from your mind," he instructed me, and I obeyed, though it wasn't easy to do. "Now, think about the transformation, how your human shape looks, how it feels. Envision it."

I did what he said and quickly felt the change begin to ripple through my body—my fur disappearing into smooth skin and my tail shrinking until I was just my usual flesh and bones self.

I gazed down at my hands and arms then up at Cody. His eyes held the promise of a night filled with pleasure, but there was something more—a sharper edge than I'd seen before, and it made my nipples hard.

It was apparent he noticed when his lips curved into a devilish grin, and he pulled me against his bare chest.

"I want you, Ember. I need to feel myself inside of you again."

A moan escaped my lips when he kissed my neck and raked his teeth across my shoulder. His cock hardened against me, and I instinctively pressed closer to him, wanting him just as much.

But he stepped back, taking his blazing heat with him. When I peeked up, and our gazes met, I was ready to lie down right where we stood and spread my legs for him. I needed him so desperately.

"Cody..."

He reached out and took my hand in his. Evidently, he had other plans. And as he led me down a familiar path that twinkled with soft, white lights, I knew my not-so-secret wish was about to come true.

CHAPTER TWENTY-THREE

EMBER

"Your wolf is incredible," Alex said excitedly as I walked through the front door behind Cody.

Alex closed the distance between, drawing me into his arms. My breath hitched. For a moment, I'd forgotten I was naked until I was pressed against him. I looked down between us and saw my cleavage was pressed tightly against his chest. When I glanced up, my face grew warm from the way he looked at me.

So much for modesty. Apparently, now that my wolf had awakened, we didn't give a shit that our boobs weren't as perky as we wished they were.

Go, us.

"I'm so happy for you. How did it feel to have her surface? Please, tell me everything."

Cody appeared behind me with a robe, which I wrapped around my shoulders and tied loosely at the front as we made our way into the living room. I sat down in the middle of the couch. Alex and Cody sank down on either side of me.

"It felt…" I thought about how best to describe the sensations I'd experienced burning through my body when I'd transformed. The potent energy that had coursed through my veins had made me feel as though there was nothing I couldn't do when I was in my wolf form. "Powerful."

The two men chuckled at my response, and Cody slid a little closer to me, his hand circling my wrist.

"Your wolf certainly made quite an appearance. No one could take their eyes off you." He ran his fingers along the underside of my wrist, and for a moment, I wondered if he could feel the pounding of my pulse. "Especially me, us." His voice was smooth and sinful.

Alex's energy encircled me as he too moved closer. For a moment, I felt as though I might lose control having two impossibly sexy men sitting so close to me. It was as though their dominant energy squeezed the air from the room.

There was also something different about the way Alex looked at me. His smile was as warm as always, but there was a harder edge to it.

Perhaps just one word, or one touch, would be enough to show them what I wanted.

Alex's fingertips ran over the silky material of my robe until he touched the inside of my elbow before sliding a little lower to my bare leg. His caress had a possessive edge to it, which made me squeeze my legs together to try and satisfy the rush of fire they'd ignited between my thighs.

"There you are," a voice behind us interrupted for a second.

I peered over my shoulder as Grayson entered the room. He was naked, his muscles tense as though he'd just spent hours in the gym. I took in every hard-packed inch of him. His chiseled good looks were tinted with more than a subtle hint of desire in the glint of his amber eyes.

Then to my surprise, he strode across the room and lifted me from the sofa, wrapping an arm around my waist, pinning me to him. I squealed as my robe opened, and my naked body slid against his. Instinctively, I rested my palms against his chest, searching for some space between us that wasn't there to find.

I had to admit, I loved the feeling of being held in the arms of this fierce man who seemed to burn as hot as lava. But at the same time, he'd never been this forward with me before, this passionate. I couldn't help but wonder if the Fallen Moon was responsible and his actions had little to do with *me*.

But when he peered down at me, his gaze traveling slowly over my breasts, before he raised his eyes to mine, I saw what seemed like desperate need, desire, and something else swimming in his amber orbs. Something I didn't quite understand.

Then I felt the unmistakable heat of his arousal against my body, and I knew, whether it was the influence of the Fallen Moon, or something else, I didn't care. I wanted him—all of him.

"Your wolf…" A cloudy expression suddenly darkened his handsome features, and for a moment, I thought he was about to drop me.

"My wolf what?" I tilted my head, looking pointedly at him, but he turned away, refusing to meet my gaze.

Then, as expected, he let me go and scrambled back several steps.

"Grayson, what's wrong?" It was Alex who spoke, and when I peeked over at him and Cody, they both wore expressions of something other than confusion.

How could they not *be as confused as I was? Why were they looking at him with some sense of understanding when he was acting so strangely?*

Grayson regarded me silently for a moment, then scowled, his eyes flashing. "You know damn well what you do to me." His voice had roughened, deepened to almost anger. It set me on edge. "It's like you're in my very blood. Like venom."

"Grayson, I don't know what you're talking about."

The heat inside of me swept over into something else, something I wasn't ready to acknowledge. And whatever it was mixed into the storm of desire that had been brewing between us since the beginning..

"So, you don't feel *anything*? Not a fucking thing?" The raw scrape of his voice made me uneasy. "If so, then you're as dead inside as your wolf was for all those years."

I blinked, flustered by the fury in his tone.

"I-I don't know what—"

The expression in Grayson's eyes cut off whatever I was about to say. They were filled with an intensity that took my breath away.

I felt like my world was spinning out of control—my nerves jumped, my body tensed, and that wicked torrent of desire threatened to carry me beyond a point of no return if I didn't back away.

Then his mouth came down on mine, hard and fast, his lips bruising mine in a demanding and possessive kiss that was filled with primal, unrestrained energy.

I gave into it as his tongue invaded my mouth, filling me with urgency and longing.

Whatever rational part of my mind I'd been trying to hold onto—at least long enough to make sure I wouldn't make a fool out of myself—vanished and was replaced by a desperate hunger, which thrashed wildly inside of me, demanding to be satisfied.

I kissed him back just as hard, wanting him to know that *yes, I felt something even if I didn't understand what* it *was.* I surrendered to him, my mouth mobile, my body lost in the smooth, sensual heat that surrounded us.

"Ember."

The way he moaned my name against my lips stirred something deep inside that made me crave him in a way I'd never imagined possible. Then his hands slid from my back to my hips until he was squeezing my ass.

I squealed when he lifted me a bit higher, and my legs wrapped tightly around his waist as we stumbled back until we bumped into a wall.

Then everything faded into the background as his mouth demanded all my attention once again. Only when he lowered his lips to my neck, and I felt his teeth graze my shoulder a little too roughly, did I dare to open my eyes.

With a sharp gasp, as though I'd maimed him, he set me down and cursed under his breath.

"You," Grayson growled as he glared at Cody. "She's meant to be *your* mate. You've said it again and again. So, why are you both here? Why haven't you claimed her yet? It's the night of the Fallen Moon. Surely your bond is so strong you can't ignore it?"

Grayson seemed as though he was on the verge of completely losing control. I worried he and Cody were moments away from getting into an all-out brawl. I didn't want to see them so worked up, especially over me. I would leave before I ever let *that* happen.

"Please, stop," I replied and then scowled at how mousey I sounded. There was no force behind my words.

I couldn't just walk away from them, though, not tonight, not when Grayson had given me a taste of what the night could be. "I don't mean to cause any—"

"I haven't claimed her because she isn't mine to claim." Cody's voice was a barely contained growl. "And she isn't yours."

My heart dropped. His words weren't ones of anger but of acceptance. He knew I wasn't ready to be claimed by anyone.

So why did I feel such tightness in my chest?

When Grayson lunged forward and Cody jumped to his feet, I almost threw myself between them to stop one from attacking the other, but Alex beat me to it, standing between them and forcing them to back off.

"Grayson, stop. This isn't helping!" He spun toward Cody. "What do you mean, she isn't *yours* to claim?"

Is this how shifters treated women? As though they were nothing more than property to be claimed, to be had, to be owned?

"No one gets to claim me," I responded as I tightened the robe around me, ensuring it didn't slip open again. "I don't know what is going on with you guys, but I don't want to be the cause of arguments. Especially over this whole *mate* thing." I focused my attention on Grayson, who looked as though he might fly across the room and rip the others to shreds.

"Besides, *you've* made it clear you don't even believe in that," I said heatedly, pointing at Grayson.

He opened his mouth to say something, but I cut him off.

"You're incredible men, *all* of you, and you've done so much for me, but I'm not a piece of meat you get to fight over. And believe me, no woman—or man—is worth losing friends over." I took a deep breath to steady my fiery nerves. "And you're more than that to each other. You're family. Not everyone is fortunate to have that, remember?" I caught the shrill sound in my voice and forced myself to calm down. "You're all lucky to have each other. You should try to remember that."

Cody crossed his arms over his bare chest. He didn't say a word, but I could tell from the expression on his face that he was still raging.

"Answer the question, Cody."

My eyebrows pinched together at Grayson's stern tone. Clearly, he wasn't willing to let things go.

Cody eyed me carefully, then took a few steps forward. "Ember isn't like any other she-wolf I've known. The Fallen Moon awakened her wolf, and yes, she was stunning. And strong. She'd rival the most powerful she-wolf in this clan. But she isn't my mate. She isn't *anyone's* mate, and I pity the man— or the shifter—who dares to tell her otherwise."

I was filled with deep appreciation for Cody's words and his understanding that even though he felt drawn to me, I couldn't give him what he wanted, what he deserved.

I wanted to say something to him, something meaningful, something to let him know how much he meant to me, but I was lost for words.

Then he stepped behind me, and I shivered when he moved my hair aside and kissed the back of my neck in that sensitive place. It sent a streak of fire through my body, making my knees weak. But somehow I managed to stay standing.

"So, I hope that answers your question, Alpha. She isn't mine to claim." His words came out in a throaty whisper, making me squirm.

I shifted backward, wanting to feel his heat against my back.

When he spoke again, his breath tickled the hair along my hairline. "She isn't anyone's to claim."

He turned me around then, until we were standing face to face. I breathed in his masculine scent and watched as his lips curved into that smile—the one that was dark and sexy around the edges—the same one that had ensnared me from the moment he came by my carnival stand and agreed to play my silly game.

His hand reached out to cradle my jaw as he slowly lifted his eyes to meet my gaze. When his fingers brushed across my skin, I nearly wept with desire and affection.

For a man who'd found me in a world I didn't belong in.

For a man who'd saved me from myself.

He eased forward, and I parted my lips in anticipation of his kiss, but his mouth landed lower. I tipped my head to the side as he traced a trail of fire over my skin, his teeth grazing my neck just enough to make me moan.

"But if I *did* claim you, I'd first make love to you," he murmured against my collarbone, his deep voice a seductive kiss just for me. "And then, right before I came in you, I would bite you..." He kissed the side of my neck, then lower to the hollow beneath my ear. "Right in this spot... here."

I felt the smooth edge of his teeth, and something thudded deep inside me. But before I could get lost in it, he lifted his face, and his teasing smile was back.

"But I can't, because like I said..." his words were whispered against my skin, "...you aren't mine to claim."

Then he stepped back, leaving my body in a raging firestorm of desperate need.

Cody was right. I was no one's to claim. I couldn't be. Not with a wolf slayer hunting me down, not when I'd bring nothing but heartache to this clan.

And not when I didn't even know where I came from or what pack I belonged to. And now that my wolf had awakened, it seemed very important.

When I'd caught my breath and gazed up at them, Alex gifted me with a warm smile, which told me what it always did —that everything would work out.

Grayson, however, looked as though he was still struggling with something, an unsettled expression on his face.

"Her wolf was much stronger than I'd anticipated," he said, finally daring to look at me. "I guess you aren't as weak as I thought. I only saw you briefly before you took off into the forest, but your wolf is worthy of being part of this clan..." His voice trailed off into nothingness.

"What Grayson is trying to say," Alex added, staring at his fellow Alpha for a second before giving me his attention once more, "is that you're welcome to stay here... with us. For good."

Tears welled up in my eyes, and I choked back a sob. I wasn't expecting that. I hadn't even considered it, not after learning of my fate.

In that moment, I'd never felt so wanted, so cared for. These three men were welcoming me into their clan, their family with open arms.

The way they looked at me stirred conflicting emotions inside me as I tried to gather my thoughts.

I had tonight. One last night to show them how I felt about them. How it could be if things were different.

And I wouldn't waste it.

CHAPTER TWENTY-FOUR

GRAYSON

I'd never wanted a woman as badly as I wanted Ember. I needed to suck, kiss, and squeeze every inch of her sexy body, to commit her taste to memory, to know every curve as though I'd had her in my bed a hundred times before.

But I was angry, *so angry*, I was breaking the one rule that had always kept me from having my heart smashed into a thousand pieces. I needed to wipe any thought of a future with her from my mind and simply enjoy fucking her.

Guilt had overwhelmed me when I'd kissed her in front of Cody. He was the one who'd first felt her energy and the connection I'd been too stubborn to acknowledge. He'd told us all along she was meant to be his, yet there I was, with my greedy hands on her ass and my tongue in her mouth.

But then when I'd turned to him, frustration clouding my judgment and making me want to rage at the injustice that I could never *have* her, I'd seen emotion in his eyes I hadn't expected.

It was a look of knowing, of acceptance, and most apparent, the look of a man who wanted the woman he loved to be happy.

Even if it meant he'd be miserable.

His expression told Alex and me that Cody would step back if it was what Ember wanted. He'd brought her to our home rather than his tonight. He must have known what she wanted.

The wicked passion dancing in the depths of her eyes made my cock stiffen. This was a woman who could possess me if I wasn't careful. I'd fucked many women before, but the way I'd felt when her robe slipped open and her beautiful tits bounced free made me want to take my time with her. To squeeze my cock inside of every place she'd allow and give her just as much pleasure.

I stood in frustration, unsure what to do with myself, whether I should sit, stand, pace the floors, or carry her to my bed caveman style. I watched her intently. We all did, mesmerized by her splendor and how she commanded attention without even trying.

Here, at her fingertips, were three men delirious with desire for her. We would've ripped each other apart if she'd asked us to.

Things like loyalty and brotherhood were meaningless words as we waited for her to choose who she wanted.

Cody had said she was no one's mate, but I refused to believe him. The look on her face when his eyes met hers told me otherwise.

Only mates could look at each other *that* way.

"I'm going to go shower," she murmured, almost impishly, as she turned toward the staircase.

My heart sank, and I nearly growled. Tonight would end like other nights before. She'd shower and slip into bed alone.

But when my downcast eyes lifted and I saw the curious smile on her face, I knew just how wrong I'd been.

"Join me?"

And when her eyes swept from Cody to Alex before resting on me, it was clear she wasn't just inviting *one* of us upstairs with her. She was asking all three of us.

Cody was the last to move, and for a second, I thought he'd reject her request, but when I peered over my shoulder, I saw the expression on his face and knew there was no way he wasn't going to have her.

We made our way up the stairs, but before we reached the top, I scooped her into my arms, causing her to squeal.

"I think we should save the shower for afterward," I murmured against her cheek as I held her delicious body in my hands.

"My wolf awakened tonight," she purred in response. "I'm filthy... just a quick shower will do."

Patience was *not* a virtue I possessed.

We made our way into the bathroom, and I set her down on the cool tile while Cody turned the water on and adjusted the temperature. Within minutes, the two of them were stepping in together, with Ember standing directly under the stream of water.

She let Cody soap up her body, his hands working a lather as he kneaded her tits and squeezed her nipples.

It made sense he was the one to help clean off the dirt and sand after they'd explored the forest together on such an important night.

Somehow him being the one felt important.

I watched her slide her wet body against his, her tits now rubbing against his chest, as he tugged her into his embrace. She tilted her face up, but his lips were already parted, his tongue searching for hers.

Their kiss started slow and soft, but as his hands skillfully moved over her lower back, then to her shoulders, and finally tangled into her hair, everything intensified. The air in the room was suddenly electric. Their movements grew more demanding and more frantic.

But I was rooted in place, my cock hard and throbbing and my heart hammering in my chest.

I hadn't shared a woman with anyone before, so I wasn't sure when to step in, but when I saw Alex had undressed, greed took over, and the restless energy burning through my body refused to wait a second longer.

I stepped forward, joining them under the mist of hot water, unsure how to get her into my arms without angering Cody but knowing it was exactly what I had to do.

A sigh escaped Ember's lips, muffled by Cody's mouth. His hand slid between her legs, circling her clit and finding its way into her pussy.

She cried out, her tangled, wet hair falling into her face as she arched against the shower wall.

Fuck, I wanted her.

Cody peered at me over his shoulder, a grin curving his lips that told me all he cared about was giving her pleasure. His expression said he welcomed whatever she wanted, whatever she needed.

He was the one to lift her up this time, and she wrapped her legs around his waist the same way she'd done with me earlier. She kissed his neck as he carefully made his way out of the shower, water splashing across the tile as he carried her toward the door, while Alex, ever so practical, grabbed a towel.

As they moved down the hallway, Ember lifted her eyes and peered over Cody's shoulder, her gaze latching onto mine, inviting me to follow. Her fingers reached out to Alex. He strode closely behind them as they finally found their way to the foot of my bed.

My bed.

He hadn't brought her into one of the many spare rooms. He'd carried her into *my* domain. *Did he realize what he was doing? That if Ember wanted me, I wouldn't stop until she was screaming my name?*

That I wasn't so sure I could share?

Cody set her down gently, and she found herself standing in the middle of the three of us, circling her like she was our prey.

I had an overwhelming desire to push her back onto the bed and slide my cock inside her, but I held back. Though it took every ounce of strength not to move a muscle.

She needed to give me permission, to tell us what she wanted.

"I can't decide," she murmured, the blue in her eyes darkening. "Who wants you more. My wolf... or me."

Her eyes danced across my body, roaming from my face down my chest until they settled on my cock, her lips curving into a smile.

It still wasn't enough. I needed her to *tell* me what she wanted. Spell it the fuck out.

Then her gaze clicked over to Alex, who offered her a towel, but she didn't seem to notice, despite his hand reaching out.

All she seemed to acknowledge was his hard, lean body.

Cody was the first to move, drawing her into his arms once again. They kissed just as feverishly as they had before, but this time, when she tore her lips away from his, she said the words I'd been waiting to hear.

"Make love to me. Please."

Her voice was breathless and filled with desire, which only made my cock harder. "I need you. *All* of you."

CHAPTER TWENTY-FIVE

EMBER

Cody's arms snaked around me possessively, and the look on his face told me he wanted to give me all the pleasure a woman could hope for, just like he'd given me when we were lying on the beach.

He kissed my neck first, his lips trailing fire across my damp skin, his teeth grazing my flesh in a way which made it clear that while he couldn't claim me as his mate, he was more than ready to claim me in another way.

The ache between my legs became almost too much to bear, and I squirmed, hoping they'd hurry up.

I didn't have long to wait.

Strong hands grabbed my ass, shifting my weight and tumbling us onto the bed. It took a moment for me to realize it was Cody as he nuzzled my neck and held me tightly against his chest. I was sitting on his lap, his cock firm against my ass, and I wondered for a brief moment if I could handle three men. If I could be so bold, so daring.

But there was no time to second-guess whether I was woman enough for three fierce and gorgeous men when Grayson shifted forward until he stood near where we sat on the mattress, watching over my shoulder as Cody's cock inched closer to my pussy.

The expression on his face told me that when it was his turn, it wouldn't be gentle or slow.

I didn't care.

Finally, Alex joined us on the bed, sitting by my side, his hands reaching out, hesitantly at first, as though he wanted to make sure this was really what I wanted.

That it was okay to touch me.

It was.

When I moaned at the wicked desire sweeping through my body because of the way they were staring at me and touching me, like I was the most beautiful woman they'd ever seen, whatever reluctance Alex had quickly vanished. He squeezed my breasts, tweaking my hard nipples. His touch was just this side of rough. And then he lowered his mouth and greedily sucked on them.

I squirmed on Cody's lap, wiggling my ass so it pressed against his cock, and the deep growl that tickled the side of my neck told me my time to tease was over.

"Fuck me. Please." I murmured, to no one in particular.

Cody lifted me from his lap, so I was lying almost sideways, and I realized he was trying hard not to be possessive, to let me have what I so desperately needed.

All of them.

Grayson took a final step forward, his knees brushing the bed. His eyes locked on mine, but there was no question in his expression, only knowing.

I longed for him to climb onto the bed and kiss me, but he bit down on his bottom lip as though deciding what he wanted to do to me first.

Then he closed the distance, the mattress sagging beneath his added weight, his hulking body crawling over me, until he hovered just above my breasts, his muscled chest glistening in the dim light. He gazed down at me with burning intensity, and I caught a glimpse of the fierce animal who rippled beneath his skin, begging to be free to play with mine.

And my wolf wanted nothing more than to answer his call when his soft tongue snaked its way between my lips and his fingers roughly tangled in my hair.

He held me tightly for a moment, as though he might lose me if he didn't. The sensation of being wanted so acutely made me moan against his mouth.

Then he lifted his body from mine, taking his heat with him. I wanted to beg him to climb back on me, but then he lay at my side. His strong hands squeezed my breasts.

"You make me so fucking horny."

He leaned closer and kissed the breath out of me while Cody settled between my legs, his fingers sliding down my stomach and between my thighs. It was his turn to tease, and I objected, but my cries were muffled by Grayson's relentless kiss—a kiss that told me just how long he'd been waiting for this moment.

Alex slid beside me, his hands caressing my shoulder. His fingers were soft. He didn't squeeze my skin the way Grayson did. Alex's stroke was sweet and gentle, the contrast between the two of them so intense while I lay in the middle.

Cody's skillful fingers quickly found their way to my clit, and when I felt the first wave of pleasure circling my body, I arched my back. Alex slipped behind me so I could lean against his broad chest, and Cody slid farther down between my legs.

"Spread your legs for us, baby," Grayson nearly growled the words as he watched Cody's mouth dip lower, his lips kissing one thigh, then the other, before his tongue found its way to my pussy.

I closed my eyes and moaned, softly at first, then louder, lost in the thrum of desire coursing through my veins. He ignited a primal need in me that demanded to be satisfied.

I opened my legs wider. Cody slid his silky tongue inside me, his mouth and fingers working to cover my clit while Grayson got to his knees. He tried to steady himself on the soft mattress, but then he grumbled in frustration when the motion around him made it next to impossible. Instead, he scooted closer, positioning the curve of his cock so it was mere inches away from my open mouth.

"So big..." There was no power behind my breathless words, only raw need and a desperate hunger to sample every inch of him. I reached out and wrapped my hand around his thick shaft, stroking the smooth, hot skin.

"You're so sexy." Grayson's tone was brusque, breaking into my haze of pleasure. "I want you so fucking bad," were his tortured words.

His cock was thick, a challenge to wrap my lips around, but I kissed the head and then slid my tongue along the base up to the tip. Finally, I took it into my mouth, inch by inch, trying hard to swallow as much as I could. He chuckled when I pulled back.

"You don't have to suck it all, baby."

But I wanted to. I craved every inch of him in my mouth. I needed to give him as much pleasure as possible. I relaxed my throat to accommodate his incredible girth, so I could suck it greedily. This time I managed to sweep my mouth along his length, my tongue lapping at the sensitive ridge.

He let out a growl, which told me he was more than a little impressed, and it drove me on as he fervently pumped his cock into my mouth.

Cody was just as relentless in his quest to make me come, his tongue flickering over my clit, lightly and slowly, bringing me wave after wave of pleasure. Then he snarled impatiently against my skin, and I knew he couldn't wait any longer.

I tilted my hips forward, ready to feel Cody bury himself deeply inside of me, but when I tore my mouth from Grayson's cock, my eyes widened when I saw that it was Alex who knelt between my legs.

He shot me a devilish grin, making me even hotter. His usual kind and gentle expression vanished, replaced with the look of a man who wanted to use me for his own pleasure.

"Fuck me, Alex," I murmured as Cody reappeared, shifting into the vacant space next to me and trailing kisses down my neck to my breasts. I groaned as he sucked on each nipple in turn, the sound of his lips popping when he pulled away.

Alex slid his cock between my thighs, rubbing it up and down, teasing my aching clit. I longed to reach down between my legs and rub my way to a climax, but when I tried, Grayson grabbed my wrist.

"Let me."

His hand slipped down, and his fingers circled my clit while my other hand reached out for his cock, then Cody's. I wanted both hands filled with them.

Grayson nearly brought me to climax as he stroked my clit with his thumb. I gasped, turning my face toward him to show my appreciation, my desire. My mouth found his cock once again, and the heat of him nearly scalded my lips.

"Fuck yeah, that's it. Suck me, Ember. Suck my cock."

A muffled cry slipped past my lips when Alex pummeled my pussy with his cock even harder, the sharp thrusts of his hips so forceful it almost hurt.

Almost.

The first wave of my climax raced through my body, the throbbing heat causing me to arch my back and moan.

"Oh, God…" I murmured when it felt like he was filling and stretching me more than ever before. Since Grayson refused to let go of my head, his cock still buried in my mouth, my words came out as nothing more than a breathless whimper.

"Alex… Cody… Grayson." Saying their names, with my mouth full of Grayson's cock, was like tasting something sinful. It was a wickedly delicious sound that clouded my mind with a dark passion.

I squeezed Cody's cock with my hand, making him pant my name. It was hard to concentrate with so much going on, but Cody seemed to be waiting patiently for my full attention.

Alex tried to decrease the force and pace of his thrusts, moaning when I moved a little faster. He begged me to slow down and mumbled something about how tight my pussy felt. But I ignored his pleas, lifting my ass off the bed so I could gain even more traction.

Two could play this game.

I needed to take him to the edge, then force him over it just as he had done to me. I hummed with the need to pleasure these men, to satisfy them fully, to let them use my body for their desires as much as I was using theirs.

Alex reached down and gripped my hips, trying to tame me, but it was too late. When I felt him thrash against me, I knew he was about to lose control.

"Come for me, Alex." My demand was muffled as I slid another inch of his cock into my mouth, going deeper than I ever thought possible, my fingers curled around the base of his shaft.

Grayson stared at me with heavy-lidded eyes "That's it, baby. So good," he groaned, willing me to suck harder, deeper.

I knew Alex had heard my words when I felt the heat of him on my thigh as his breathing sped up and he moaned one last time.

Suddenly my body was being repositioned as Grayson slid his cock from my mouth and got to his feet. I tried to follow him with my gaze, but then Cody's mouth came down on mine, hard, his tongue teasing against my lips, and I was swept away in the familiar feel of his embrace as he moved on top of me.

"I need you," he growled against my mouth, his hands palming my breasts, my nipples responding to his touch. "Can I have you, Ember?"

I wiggled beneath him, and he pressed into me harder, his

hips pinning me to the mattress. My body was on fire as I arched against him, against this man who'd made me come alive, made me feel so loved.

"I'm yours, Cody."

My pussy stretched to accept his cock, his blue eyes glued to my face as though he wanted to see what he did to me—what his cock did to me.

Frantically, I reached out, searching for the headboard, but I was too far from the top of the bed as I met him stroke for stroke, his thrusts letting me how good I was making him feel.

Then he lowered his head, and his mouth encircled my nipple with rough sweetness, and I cried out, head flung back as I stared hazily up at the ceiling.

I'm going to come... I need to come.

I didn't realize I'd said those words aloud until Cody's brusque, yet soothing, voice rumbled against my ear, telling me, "Not yet... I'm not done with you."

Then I was being tugged, my body turned, and I found myself lying on my stomach, my cheek flat against the fluffy mattress.

I felt so exposed this way, so vulnerable, and a thrill of pleasure coursed through me. I'd never been so free with a man before—let alone with *three* men. As his hands reached for my wrists, holding my arms behind me, he slid his cock back into my pussy. I whimpered his name and begged him to make me come.

"Your pussy feels so good around my cock," Cody groaned, adjusting my body so I was practically on my knees. "Too good."

Alex was back in my line of sight, the devilish gleam still in his eyes as he stroked my hair and kissed my face while Cody fucked me hard and steady, his hips thrashing against me, his balls slapping my pussy.

Someone reached around and rubbed my clit, helping to

relieve the ache. When I lifted my heavy lids, I saw it was Grayson.

Everything went still for a heartbeat, and then I cried out, as Grayson's fingers moved in steady, smooth strokes. Cody finally let go of my wrists, and my arms flailed out, grabbing for Alex, reaching for Grayson. The three of them filled my body with liquid desire. I bucked violently against Cody while Alex captured my moans in his mouth with a searing kiss.

I struggled for breath as I spiraled out of control, my orgasm fiercer than I was prepared for. I caught a blurred glimpse of Grayson before his roving mouth was on my neck and shoulders, exploring, playing, biting. Another breathless moan erupted from me when strong hands squeezed my ass hard. Then a palm came down with a sharp crack. There was a moment of reprieve before I found myself spiraling into a world of pleasure, where I lost myself completely.

Cody pulled his cock from me, and I moaned in protest. It wasn't fair. I wasn't done. I hadn't had enough. Not yet.

But when I peered over my shoulder and saw the sated look on his face, I knew I'd pushed him too hard, too far. His shoulders were lifting and falling as he caught his breath. When he peered up at me, my lips curved into a smile at the flushed look of satisfaction on his face.

"My turn." Grayson's voice was rough, and full of demand, the thrumming vibration going straight to my nipples. He slid back on the bed until he was leaning flat against the headboard, then he rested his arms along the edge of it, his hard cock jutting out, inviting me to play.

As I slid up the mattress toward him, I nearly groaned in desire at the sight of his undeniably dominant appearance. His hair was slightly tousled in a way that made me want to rake my fingers through it some more. It turned me on to know I was the cause of its current messy appearance.

"Come on, baby," he murmured, his gaze locked on mine. "I've been waiting too long."

His body was a wall of hard-packed muscle, and I took in every inch of him as I slowly crawled forward to meet him. His cock had felt so good in my mouth; its thick girth difficult to wrap my mouth around. I shuddered with pleasure at the thought of my wet, aching pussy being challenged as well.

It was a challenge I was eager to accept.

"Save the best for last?" His smirk was tinged with a hint of devil-may-care.

I crept between his legs, then slithered my body over his, my breasts smooshing against his hard chest while he kept his hands gripping the headboard, allowing me to do whatever I wished with his body. To use him for my pleasure.

I kissed his chest, my lips leaving a wet trail as I worked my way to his neck. When I got there, he took a shuddering breath, and I knew I'd found his weak spot.

I smirked when he turned his face, and his gaze met mine, his eyes giving me a warning I was far too happy to ignore. I could handle whatever he sent my way.

He let go of the headboard, and his arms snaked around me, pulling me in roughly. His lips found mine. His kiss wasn't a gentle one filled with a promise of forever. It was the kiss of a man who wanted to leave his mark, to make me forget any other who'd come before him.

My pussy buzzed with the need to be pleasured as I climbed onto his lap and rocked against him, his cock filling the space between my thighs and making me tremble with desire.

"Oh, God," I groaned, my breath huffing out in a rush when the head of his cock pushed against my slit. I adjusted my weight, sitting on the balls of my feet, and pressed down, this time going further, as deep as I dared go until his shaft was buried inside of me.

"Oh, fuck! Grayson!"

I couldn't stop the screams that tore from my lips or the way I kept repeating them as I accepted every inch of his cock. His eyes darkened as he filled me with its brutal thickness. I squirmed in protest at first, but I soon found myself lost in the blissful torture of his body inside mine.

He held me tight, moaning beneath me, his hands clutching my lower back, and his face buried in my shoulder. His words were nothing but a string of whispered tones against my skin, but he wasn't saying anything that demanded an answer.

We were lost in our pleasure, in the powerful need that rippled over our skin and glued our bodies together.

"Fuck," Grayson groaned, his lips finding my jawline, trailing kisses down my neck. "You make my cock so hard."

"And you make me so wet," I whispered as I leaned back, so I could touch my clit while I bounced on his cock.

My eyes drifted closed against the dark flush of arousal. I rode his cock as though it was made for me, intensifying my thrusts as his hips lifted to meet mine.

When he'd had enough of me being in control, he scooped me up into his arms and pushed me onto my back. I was unable to keep myself from moaning when he pushed back into me, my pussy vibrating around his invading cock.

I wanted more—all of it, every inch of him deep inside of me. Instinctively, I thrust against him, arching my back and lifting my hips from the bed as a signal I wanted as much as he wanted to give. He answered, stretching me open and filling me up until my vision blurred.

"Oh, Grayson," I gasped, unprepared for the astonishing pleasure of feeling him fully inside of me.

His hips moved like pistons, and I went limp with bliss as I surrendered to all he had to give me—all I'd asked for.

"Baby," he breathed, his voice hoarse, almost strangled, as though he was weakened by his hunger for me. "I need to come."

The intensity became too much, and moments later, I

opened my mouth in a soundless squeal as my pussy clenched and released continuously around his cock in a furious climax.

"Oh, fuck!" I panted as Grayson swiped a lock of hair away from where it was plastered to my sweaty temple.

"That's it, baby. Come for me." He stared deeply into my eyes as he drove me over the edge, leaving me a breathless, panting mess. "Come for me, Ember."

The sound of his voice was suddenly very far away as I found myself lost in my own pleasure. My body thrummed as I cried out his name. My skin was on fire, and I trembled furiously as an intense orgasm rocketed through my body.

He continued to thrust into me, moving faster with every stroke, picking up speed, which I quickly matched as I pushed back. His lips curved into a sexy grin as one of his hands wandered up to caress my breast, palming the nipple as Cody suddenly appeared and squeezed the other, the two of them working in tandem.

Alex was now on my other side, his hands tracing lines up my body and around my nipples until they reached my face, his fingers sliding over my lips. I opened my mouth as he slid one inside, and I sucked on it as I continued to come.

Ragged breaths tumbled from my lungs, but I managed to cry out one more time, the names of all my lovers dancing from my lips.

And with his next breath, Grayson stiffened and pushed into me once more, holding himself there, his muscles tight, hands now gripping my hips. He threw his head back, his muscled body rocking gently against mine before he withdrew his cock from me and rode the final waves of his orgasm.

We collapsed, sated and exhausted. Cody tugged me half on top of him, my heart pounding against his, our legs languidly tangled, and my head tucked beneath his chin. I blissfully melted against him as he stroked my hair. Alex positioned himself next to us and rested a lazy hand across my lower back.

Grayson left the room, and I heard water running. He returned moments later and climbed into the empty space on the other side of me and Cody. He wrapped his arm around my waist.

There was no need for words, only gentle caresses as we lay together.

Tomorrow would bring the promise of danger, and I'd have to face it alone. But tonight, I'd sleep in the arms of two glorious Alphas and a beta who'd stolen my heart.

CHAPTER TWENTY-SIX

EMBER

W hen I woke, wrapped in a tangle of arms and legs, I knew what I had to do.

Cinderella called, and she wanted her shoe back.

The night before would be one I'd always remember. Even now, when I closed my eyes, I could still feel their lips on my body and their hands squeezing my curves. But that was all I would allow myself—one incredible night.

So, with the morning sun, the spell had been broken, though magic still flowed through my veins, and I almost shuddered at the power of it.

What they'd told me had been confirmed. I was a wolf—a beautiful, smoky gray and dark blue wolf. The adrenaline that had streamed through my body when she'd finally surfaced had been nothing short of intoxicating. Still, I couldn't help but think about how this all began.

Wolf slayer.

The words surfaced as I thought about what I had to do. Whoever had summoned a creature from the shadow realm to come after me wouldn't stop until they'd succeeded. Elgin had told me as much, and I believed him.

Cody, Grayson, and Alex had done so much for me in the short time we'd known one another. I wouldn't repay them by bringing a murderous creature into their realm. If this beast was on the hunt for me, I refused to lead it here.

It was my turn to protect them.

I wasn't sure where I'd go or what direction I'd head in. I hadn't thought that far ahead. What I did know was from the moment I'd transformed into my wolf, one decision had been made for me.

I would *never* step foot in the cruel human world again. I'd find my way through this world of magic, and I would discover where I came from.

Who I came from.

Where I truly belonged.

And if I led danger to *that* doorstep, it was something I could live with. After all, they'd left me and my wolf to fend for ourselves our entire lives. Trying to help me defeat a wolf slayer was the least they could do.

I shook my head—enough wallowing in self-pity. Spending all those years on my own wasn't the worst thing. Everyone had lost something precious to them. Whether family, friend, or simply their youth—everybody had a reason to feel sorry for themselves.

But where did that get anyone?

Where had it ever gotten me?

As I inched toward the foot of the bed, something else popped into my mind—and the thought brought a smile to my lips.

I'd never be alone again. I had my wolf.

I slid out of Grayson's bed as quietly as I could. But trying to sneak out of a room with three men wrapped around me wasn't the easiest thing to do. Somehow, I managed it, moving slowly, inch by inch, until I was standing up, staring down at them.

They were truly magnificent, their hard bodies sprawled out

on the enormous mattress. And as I watched Cody's chest rise and fall, his gorgeous profile made me want to pepper him with kisses. I had to swallow down my emotions which threatened to wake them all.

Cody, the man who'd bared his heart and soul to me, who'd brought me from a world I didn't belong in, into one of magic… it was because of him that my wolf had finally awoken.

Alex… the sweet Alpha with a gentle spirit. A man who deserved all the happiness in the world. Together, he and Grayson made the perfect team—a blend of kindness and compassion with the power of lightning.

Grayson. What could I say about the giant of a man with a heart of gold and an intensity that made my body burn with desire? The possessive way he'd kissed me when Alex and Cody had taken turns igniting my body with more pleasure than I'd ever felt had left me breathless.

I would never forget them.

Turning, I crept back to my room and got dressed quickly, making sure to leave everything just as I'd found it. I didn't even take the time to brush out my hair. I just gathered it into a ponytail and pulled it tight.

I'd be gone within the hour, with no trace I was ever here.

Silently, I made my way downstairs and toward the front door when a shimmering object caught my eye. I turned in search of what was flashing off in the distance. There was a large bookcase at the back of the room. As I moved closer, I spotted what had caught my attention.

There was an array of trinkets placed carefully along a few of the shelves. Twinkling charms, silver and golden baubles of various sizes, and what looked like a large, crystal block with intricate carvings.

I picked it up and examined it closely. It was quite lovely. As I brought it closer to my face, I could make out the outline of two gray and silver wolves, both with emerald eyes.

Eyes that reminded me of Alex.

I turned it over, scanning the base for any markings, and found a tiny scribble of golden lettering etched into the block. I squinted, trying to make out the words, but they were too small to read.

I thought about what Alex had told me about how his brother had disappeared after their father demanded he marry someone he didn't love. There was such a deep sadness in Alex's voice when he'd mentioned Jackson, but there was also a glimmer of hope.

I wished with all my heart he'd find his brother one day, and the two would be reunited. Perhaps, I'd encounter him on my travels and convince him to return home.

Now, it was my turn to leave this world for an adventure into my past, my history. I knew this wasn't the clan I was born into. I felt it in every fiber of my being.

When my wolf had surfaced, she'd howled at the moon—a cry for the ages. But it wasn't just for the years she'd been forced to stay silent. It was a call to our people, to our clan.

And together, my wolf and I would find them.

I placed the crystal block back on the shelf and headed out the front door, closing it quietly behind me.

It was time to go.

I gazed off in the distance, trying to figure out what direction to take. I didn't exactly have a well-thought-out plan, choosing to let my instincts lead the way.

I wondered, briefly, if I should try to shift so I could cover more ground but also because the wolf inside of me refused to be ignored. She'd enough of that for one lifetime, and I could feel her growing stronger with every step I took.

She wanted to run through the nearby trees, to kick up the dirt and—

I felt the rumblings of her, so I fell to the ground, my head tucked down, my back arched as she took control. I didn't even have time to get undressed. The shift came faster than it had the night before. It was equally exhilarating.

I stretched as the transformation continued, feeling her raw energy filling every inch of my frame—my feet turning into strong paws tipped with sharp claws, my lips drawing wide to become a muzzle, which wanted to howl in appreciation of being free once again.

But it wasn't the time for that, and my wolf agreed as I made my way back in the direction of the portal, a plan taking shape in my mind.

Somehow, my wolf knew where to go. She didn't need a map or compass. She sensed something and allowed the pull to guide us as the clan grounds quickly became nothing more than a blur in the distance.

With every step, I was further away from the three men who'd been so kind to me.

Leaving them behind would wreck me, and I knew it.

My wolf picked up speed, her paws barely touching the dirt as we cleared one meadow only to end up in another. The miles stretched on with only grass and flora as far as the eye could see.

We were in our element, anchored to nature. From the tip of my whiskers to the end of my tail, I reveled in the feel of the soft grass beneath my feet and the smell of pine and wildflowers invading my senses.

But as I drew closer to the end of the grassland, something changed. The scent of wildflowers and birds was replaced by a foreign one—much more potent yet somehow familiar.

If a scent could exemplify power, I imagined this was what it would smell like.

I slowed my pace as I crested the hill. The aroma grew stronger when I saw what was ahead. Only a short distance away was a horde of wolves and men.

I moved swiftly, darting off to the side and into the fullness of the forest lining the meadow. I hid from sight and then slowly peered out. There were at least fifty men and just as many wolves.

I stiffened in fear. They looked determined, their bodies plowing forward at a mighty pace as if heading into battle. Something told me it was exactly what they were doing. They were prepared to fight.

Were they going to attack the Thunder Cove clan? Or were they part of the pack merely returning home?

Suddenly I was faced with a whole other dilemma besides finding my way through this realm into the next. *Should I stay hidden until they'd made their way past me and then make a run for it? Or should I go back and warn the guys they may be on the verge of being attacked?*

If I went back, my growing attachment to them threatened to get in the way, and I couldn't afford to let that happen. I had to keep danger from darkening their doorstep.

Then the memory of their touch resurfaced. I could still feel the weight of their lips when they'd captured mine. Still feel how my body ignited in a blaze of passion when they'd made love to me.

My wolf was as torn as I was. We wanted to charge forward and discover where we came from, but we also wanted to protect those who'd helped her surface, to warn those who'd given me so much.

I closed my eyes for just a second, wanting to steady myself and think clearly. But when I opened them again and saw the enemy was getting closer, I knew in my heart I couldn't leave without warning them.

Let's go!

I didn't have to tell my wolf twice. I took off back in the direction I'd come, running as fast as my legs could carry me.

The knowledge that men were fast approaching filled me with terror. I knew I had no choice. I had to get to Alex, Grayson, and Cody before the oncoming army did.

CHAPTER TWENTY-SEVEN

EMBER

I t seemed to take forever to get back onto clan grounds, but finally, I topped the last hill that would lead to their territory.

"Stop!"

I cocked my head in the direction of the voice but refused to stop running. Adrenaline pumped through my veins, propelling me forward at a speed I didn't think was possible.

"I said stop!"

A man suddenly appeared at my side, tackling me to the ground. I hit the dirt hard, my body crushed under his weight as I tried to fight him off, but when he wrapped his arms around me, I knew I was no match for him, especially when my wolf withdrew and my body shrank. My fur bristled before turning into smooth skin.

"Let me go!" I squirmed under his control, but he was too heavy. I needed to get out from under him before I suffocated. Panic tore through me at the thought of him accidentally crushing me with his massive frame.

"I need to warn them!"

Despite my pleas, the man refused to let go. I kicked and

swung my body from side to side, desperately trying to escape, but he quickly overpowered me as though I was nothing more than a paper doll.

Finally, I got a good look at him and realized the man who held me captive beneath his hulking frame was no stranger at all.

"Rylen, oh my God, people are coming! Wolves… men. Lots of them. We need to warn everyone."

I expected him to release me immediately, but that thought quickly dissipated when he turned to me, his gaze darkening, and I was reminded of his words to me the night before when he wished me luck and told me I'd need it.

"They should've never brought you here. They aren't considering the future of the clan. About what this would do to us."

"Rylen, what are you…" I stole a breath as his bulky frame lifted momentarily, but it quickly lowered again and pinned my naked body to the ground.

What had I ever done to him?

"Half-breeds should be destroyed. They're like parasites… they'll infect a clan and kill it from the inside out," he continued, practically spitting out his words as he glared at me with murder in his eyes. "I won't let you *ruin* my family. Grayson and Alex need to choose mates who are worthy… like my sister or any other full blood. Not… *you.*" He practically spat the last word out as he glared down at me. "The clan wants you gone, and I'm going to make sure that happens."

One word surfaced as I fought for breath and bravery to keep fighting as his hand wrapped around my throat and squeezed.

Hatred.

Rylen didn't just dislike me. He hated me.

I'd seen hatred before. The foster parents who took me in had resented me. Loathed my presence and the things they believed I represented.

The unwanted. The unworthy.

But I'd learned many years ago to let it roll off my shoulders. After all, they detested me for things I had no control over—for decisions I hadn't made for myself.

I hadn't asked to be born. I hadn't asked to be abandoned.

And I hadn't asked to be a wolf. Or a *half-wolf.*

But now that I'd met her, I was proud of her. She wasn't inferior. She wasn't going to be silenced. She was going to fight back and stand her ground.

I kicked my legs out, connecting with a part of Rylen's body that made him bellow in pain before he scrambled to regain his control over me. I had less than seconds to respond, landing another kick, this time to his stomach.

I knew I was no match for him, but a lifetime of anger at being oppressed surfaced as I thrashed against him.

He didn't know anything about me other than I wasn't a full-blooded wolf, and somehow that was reason enough for him to want to hurt me.

I managed to squeeze out from beneath him long enough to gulp down a breath before he swung around and barreled his chest against mine, the veins in his neck bulging as his body shook in rage.

"You'll pay for that, half-breed," he growled as he momentarily lost his grip again, but he recovered quickly, this time lifting me to my feet, his hands on my wrists, pinning my arms down to my side.

"Rylen, please. I want to warn them. Then I'll go. I was already leaving!"

He lowered his face to my neck and ran his teeth over the sensitive arch of my shoulder before nearly biting my skin. The way he touched me suddenly took a strange turn, and I felt more vulnerable than before.

"I'd prefer to kill you and be done with it, but the Alpha of the Silver Creek Clan seems to have a deep interest in you. It'll be good for him to owe me a favor when the time comes."

He yanked my arms behind me, forcing a cry from my lips as pain seared up my arm, and I was sure something was about to break.

"Grayson and Alex might think of them as our sworn enemies, but they're saving us. From you."

I heard the pounding of heavy feet as the pack came into view. Rylen took a few steps forward, dragging me along with him. The way his chest pressed up against my back and the way he slid his hands around my chest made me want to cry out. I wished he'd pin me down on the ground and suffocate me rather than hold me this way.

Shift, dammit. Why are you hiding again?

I tried to tap into my newly found power, but my wolf refused. I wasn't surprised. I'd barely awakened her, and now, we were already in grave danger.

"There they are. Finally." Rylen chuckled darkly. "I wonder what their fascination is with you. Maybe their Alpha has a fetish for halflings."

My pulse spiked in fear as men surrounded us. Wolves lined the outside of the crowd to protect those who made up the center, but as I watched in horror, wondering what was about to happen to me, the mass divided, and Rylen shoved me forward before he released his grip on me. I fell to the ground.

"That's enough, Rylen," a voice growled from the midst of the crowd. "Our Alpha will take it from here."

"Just make sure she never returns," Rylen barked back as he wiped the sweat from his brow. "My Alphas deserve better than this imposter."

My eyes darted around frantically, trying to get a sense of the situation from my low vantage point. Everywhere I looked, men hovered over me, the sun on their backs, their faces wreathed in shadows.

"Don't be afraid," a deep, commanding voice said as the crowd parted, and a man stepped forward. "We won't hurt you."

One of the men standing next to him passed him something. He leaned down and handed it to me. "Here, put this on."

To my surprise and relief, it was a type of cloak. I'd never been more grateful as I covered myself with the shimmering silver and cream material, which smelled of fresh air and lavender.

"You're safe now. We're bringing you home."

It took me a minute to find my voice. "Home?"

"Yes," he replied. "To the Silver Creek clan. To your people."

The silhouette reached out a hand to help me to my feet. I couldn't see more than an outline of a tall and well-built frame, but as the man came closer, I recognized the shape of his face.

I reached for him but paused at the memory of when he'd first held my hand. When we'd touched, the strange flow of energy had left my mind a scattered mess and blurred my vision.

But now, as he stood before me, his image was sharper than ever. I eyed him carefully before my gaze finally rested on the patch embroidered into the collar of his shirt.

It was a triangle crest with a silver tree and pink leaves that wove their way around each branch. I'd seen the same image before when we'd first met as the vision had overtaken me.

"Dawson."

A smile ghosted his lips as my gaze slid from the patch on his shirt up to his gray eyes, touched by storm clouds.

"I'm so happy to see you again, Ember."

This time, his expression wasn't one of concern like it was when he'd found me at the carnival. It was the look of a man who could feel my power as if it were his own.

The power of my wolf.

I allowed him to help me to my feet, and his men surrounded us protectively.

"Are you ready? The gateway to my realm isn't far."

I nodded wordlessly as he offered his arm, and I banded mine around it.

I wasn't sure what awaited me beyond the portal, but somehow I knew what he said was true.

I was going home.

ABOUT CATE CASSIDY

Cate Cassidy is an 80's movie buff who is addicted to coffee and tales of magic and mayhem.

Fun fact: She has watched *Can't Buy Me Love* 11 times and *Pretty in Pink* more times than she can count. #TeamDuckie

Cate lives near the ocean in Atlantic Canada with her attention-seeking Bengal, Darwin, who occasionally moves off the keyword long enough for her to write a chapter or two.

Printed in Poland
by Amazon Fulfillment
Poland Sp. z o.o., Wrocław
20 April 2021

402dfc5e-197f-4387-a581-d4c426aa4e5aR01